TEXAS TWOSOME

ROMANCE ACROSS STATE LINES

DEBBIE WHITE

Editing by Leo Bricker of The Grammatical Eye

Cover Design by Larry White

❀ Created with Vellum

CHAPTER 1

*H*er heels clicked down the long hallway as she made her way to the pool of desks that made up the magazine's editorial group, smiling and waving as she went along. She pulled open her bottom drawer and tossed in her Michael Kors purse that she'd bought from a small and expensive boutique in Las Vegas, and turned on her computer. While the computer went through all the latest updates, she walked over to the coffee station with her "I love New York" coffee mug and filled it up, topping it with not two, but three creamers. She gave it a whirl with a stirring stick and then promptly spun around to head back to her desk.

Bam! Coffee went flying everywhere.

"Watch where you're going," she screamed, hot coffee dripping down her brand-new cream-colored blouse from Neiman Marcus.

"I'm sorry, I looked down for just a moment," the man said.

She stared at him. He was dripping coffee from his tie. "Who are you?" she blurted.

He wiped his hand on his slacks and then offered it to her. "Jack. Jack Porter," he said.

A frown quickly replaced her dropped jaw. She slowly reached out and took his hand. "Rebecca Parsons. If you'll excuse me, I have to run to the bathroom and see if I can salvage my blouse. I hope the next time we meet it won't be over spilled coffee."

Once in the restroom, she took off her blouse, and clad in her camisole, began blotting and rinsing the stained garment. It would take a bus and the metro just to get to her apartment. Sadly, she was going to be wearing coffee for the rest of the day.

Dressed again in her now wet and blotchy blouse, she made her way back to her desk. Jessica, her co-worker gasped. Rebecca put up her hand to silence her. "Don't ask. It's a long story." She plopped down into her chair.

Jessica winced at her tone. "Sorry," she said. "I have some of those little travel-sized stain remover packets. Would you like one?"

Rebecca shot her a look. "I doubt it will help. The stain has set in. This is my new blouse, too," she said, almost whimpering.

Jessica turned back to her computer and began working again.

Rebecca pulled her chair in closer and began the research for her next assignment. She was being sent to some little Texas town. "By the way, who is Jack Porter?"

"He's our new editorial chief."

She gulped. "Seriously? I just shouted at my new boss?" She chewed her bottom lip.

"I hear he's a super nice guy. Maybe if you apologize …" Jessica said.

"It was his fault. He was right up on me. I turned around and *wham*. He got it honestly," she added. "So, what happened to our old boss?"

Just then Rebecca's phone rang on her desk. She turned to answer it. "Yes, sir, I'll be right there." She hung up the receiver. "I'm going to get fired," she said as she pushed back her chair.

"Fired! What are you talking about?"

"That was Jack Porter. He wants to see me in his office right now."

Jessica widened her eyes and took in a big mouthful of air. "Good luck," she squeaked out.

Rebecca made her way to Jack's office. She lightly tapped on the door and waited.

"Come in," he bellowed.

Trembling just a little, she entered the office and began to ramble her apology, the one she told Jessica she wouldn't give. "Listen, I want to start off by telling you how sorry I am that I yelled at you. It's just that—"

He held up a hand to silence her. "Sit down, Rebecca

Parsons," he said, motioning her to sit in a chair near his desk.

Swallowing down her nerves, she sat. She smoothed out her clothes then clasped her hands in her lap. Trying to crack a smile, she wet her dry lips by running her tongue across her mouth.

"I want to apologize for ruining your pretty blouse. I'm very sorry we met like we did." He took out a check-book from the middle drawer of his desk. "So, if you tell me how much it would cost to replace your blouse, I'll write you a check." He held the pen, ready to write.

She stammered a bit. "It was on sale," she said, wincing and shrugging her shoulders. "I made a bigger deal out of it than it was. I'm sorry, Mr. Porter."

"How much would it cost to replace it today?"

"Forty-nine dollars and ninety-nine cents."

He quickly wrote something and then tore the check out and handed it to her across the desk. "Again, my apologies. I take it this will take care of it?"

She took the check and glanced at it. He'd written it for one hundred dollars. "This is too much, Mr. Porter," she protested.

"Maybe you can still salvage this one with the coffee stain by taking it to the dry cleaners." He pushed back his chair and stood up.

She followed his lead and did the same. He extended his hand to her, and she took it, shaking it gently. His hands were so soft.

"Let's try this again. My name is Jack Porter," he said, holding her hand.

"Rebecca. Rebecca Parsons," she said, holding on to his hand. He tilted his head and was about to speak when she continued. "But my friends call me Becca."

"Ahh, good to know. I hope we'll be friends," he said, coming around from his desk and walking her to the door. "I hear you're off on assignment soon," he added, opening the door.

She nodded. "Steam, Texas." She walked out and turned to face him.

He had one hand on the door, ready to close it. "An unsolved disappearance took place there many years ago."

"Yes, I'm just starting my research."

"We've interviewed the sheriff before, at another magazine that I worked for, *Police Matters in Small Town, U.S.A.*," Jack said, lowering his gaze to her coffee stained blouse.

"Well, this is the anniversary, and apparently they have this festival every year at this time. I'm just going out, taking a couple of pictures, and chatting with the sheriff. It's for our annual looking back issue. I'm sure there are no new details on the case, but hey, I've never been to Steam, Texas." She shrugged and then smiled.

He ran his hand along his chin. "If I recall correctly, the town was named after the steam engine that used to come through town."

"All I know is that I'll have to drive a couple of hours from Dallas. I plan to stop at the big mall and do some shopping. So, all will not be lost."

Jack laughed. "Maybe you'll find a replacement blouse." He tipped his head toward her stained blouse.

Becca bid Jack a good day, and then walked back to her desk in a bit of a daze. *Why was she the last one to know that they had a new boss?* Apparently, she'd been a bit preoccupied with her personal life and hadn't kept up with the changes happening in her office.

"Well, that went a lot better than I expected," Becca told Jessica.

"Like I said, I've heard he was a good guy."

"He not only paid for a replacement blouse, but he paid for my dry cleaning for the next month!"

Jessica widened her eyes. "Wow. Maybe I should bump into him. I hear he's single," she sang.

Becca pursed her lips. "I've got enough trouble with my personal life. I don't need to add dating the boss to it. But seriously, what happened to our last boss? I mean, I was only gone to Chicago for two days."

"It happened so darn fast. I heard rumors that he was stealing money or misusing the funds from the travel expense account." Jessica tipped her head as she twisted her mouth.

"Ahh. Well, I didn't really like him all that much, either," Becca said curtly.

"Either? You mean, as in you don't like Jack?" Jessica

asked.

"I don't know. He seems a bit—"

Jessica cut her off. "Boss-like?" She broke out in a wide grin then giggled.

"Whatever. I'm on my way to Steam, Texas. That's the big news of the day," Becca said, clearly changing the subject.

"Steam, Texas? Better you than me."

"What's your next assignment?" Becca typed a few things on her keyboard and stared at her monitor.

"I get to go to some little town in Alaska."

Becca spun her head toward Jessica. "Alaska?"

Jessica nodded.

"I hear it's beautiful. Have fun and take a lot of pictures. What's the story you're covering?" Becca folded her hands in her lap. Jessica had piqued her interest.

"It's actually quite interesting. Some gold mining crew was in town, and the last time they were seen was inside a bar, drinking and playing cards. Their trucks were found, but they never were."

Becca blinked a few times. "It seems more people have disappeared off the face of the earth, than you'd think. The story I'm covering is similar. Some little boy came home to find both his mom and dad gone. The windows were wide open, curtains flapping in the breeze, and a tea kettle on the stove was whistling away."

Texas, Alaska, wherever—it didn't really matter to Becca, she loved the travelling aspect of her fairly new job. She'd started out as the receptionist while she went to college majoring in, what else, journalism. After she'd worked in that position for almost a year, she finally got her much anticipated promotion to picture editor, which was followed by working as a proofreader. But the job she'd had her eye on from the very beginning was that of a writer. She'd only been in this position for a few years. It was pretty powerful to essentially be your own boss. Granted, the editor in chief had final say on what was actually printed in the magazine, but so far, she'd been pretty lucky with her submissions being accepted with only minor changes. This Jack Porter guy gave her the impression he might be a bit harder to please. Time would tell.

She was just happy to be going somewhere to get away from the drama that still plagued her since her recent breakup. Jessica had tried to tell her that he wasn't good for her, but she was hardheaded. Sometimes she wished she could talk to her mother about these things, but that was such a laughing matter.

Becca's life growing up had been anything but idyllic —drinking and partying, followed by a lot of yelling and fighting, usually ending with a call to the police by some very well-intentioned neighbors—or at the very least, nosey ones. Most days, she'd just hung her head in shame during the long walk to school. Living in the suburbs, everyone seemed to know something about you, even if you tried to hide it. The police cars driving up to the house with sirens blaring and lights flashing gave it away —every time.

She sighed whenever she thought about her very dysfunctional youth. It had been during the summer between tenth and eleventh grade that her parents had divorced. Talk about a summer killjoy. There went all the plans for Coney Island, the beach, and the camping trip her dad had planned.

Soon after the divorce was final, her mom had met Ralph. Good old Ralph. Becca used to make faces in the bathroom mirror when she'd pronounce his name. She'd pretend she was barfing in the sink when she would say Ralph, and then she'd laugh her butt off. She didn't like him at all, and when he'd approached the subject of what to call him, she'd politely told him it would not be *Dad*.

Then, after their nine months of marriage hadn't worked out, her mom had kicked him out and began dating again. Her divorce hadn't even been final yet when she'd met prospective husband number three. Becca had to think really hard to remember his name. Ah yes, Carson.

Carson could have been a good catch, but he, too, wasn't divorced and was just playing the field—testing the waters. He'd gone back to his wife, leaving Becca's mother brokenhearted. Not too broken up though, because one night she'd brought home some guy who actually did become husband number three.

Becca could see early on the pattern her mother was

developing with these husbands. She hadn't wanted any part of it and had made that clear to her mother and to the men. She'd stuck her nose in her school books, had graduated at the top of her class, and armed with a scholarship, had headed off to college, never once looking back.

Her dad and brother were MIA. The last time anyone had heard from them, they were in Canada. Or was it California? She'd lost track. She shook her head when she thought about her crazy family.

Oh, sure, she'd call her mom every now and then to say hi, but the angst she felt just dialing her number set Becca back for a few minutes until she could gather her strength and level her breathing to a non-hyper state. The phone calls never lasted more than three or four minutes.

Petite in stature, with long blonde hair highlighted with copper streaks and a complexion that was flawless, her looks were rather stunning. However, it was her crystal blue eyes that most people commented on. Even though Becca had turned a few heads in her college years, she really hadn't been that interested in forming a long-lasting relationship, probably something she had learned from her mother. She had gone on the occasional date, though, and after graduation and landing her first paid job, when she finally didn't have to make one box of cereal last for an eternity or eat ramen quite so often, she had met this guy. You know the type—tall, great build, handsome with rugged features, great hair, and bedroom eyes. Yep, that kind. The one virtue he didn't have? He didn't know how to treat women. She lacked confidence and self-esteem and didn't see it coming. Or if she did, she chose to ignore it.

Finally, after putting up with his conniving ways for much too long, she put an end to it.

"Hey, Becca," Jessica said.

Thankful for the disruption so she could stop thinking about her sadness, Becca swirled her chair around to face her friend.

"Want to go to the bar tonight and grab a cold one?"

Jessica was older than Becca, but they seemed to be compatible enough. She liked to go out on the town, guzzle down a few beers, and on some nights, they'd dress up and enjoy some fine dining and cocktails as well—just the two of them. Jessica hadn't had the best of luck with men either.

"Sure, sounds good."

Becca finished all her preliminary items for her travel plans to Steam and then logged off her laptop. Removing it from the docking station, she packed everything she'd need while away in her black leather computer travel bag.

The two women hailed a cab, and soon were bellied up to a bar, chugging down a couple of cold ones while they talked about men, family, and life.

"Maybe I'll find a hunk of a guy while in Alaska." Jessica's eyes gleamed with naughtiness.

"If you do, leave him there."

Jessica arched her brows. "That wouldn't help me if I left him there."

"Just have fun with him while you're there then leave him where you found him." Becca tipped her head then picked up her frosty mug and drew in a long taste of the ale.

"I hear you. I wish I could find a guy who knows what he wants. You know, someone who is mature, but who has been around the block a few times, so he's ready to settle down. I'm done with playing games."

Becca placed her mug down with a thud. "That."

"I still think the guys here are just after one thing. After they get it, they move on. It's just a big meat market here." Jessica watched as the cute bartender came closer. She gave him a sexy smile.

Becca jabbed her with her finger. "Stop that."

"He's pretty cute."

"Yep, and he's about twenty-five years old, too. Talk about a player. He'd love to get his hands on a thirty-nine-year-old woman."

Jessica face-palmed while staring at Becca. "Thirty-eight."

"Okay, thirty-eight, but your birthday is next month." She raised her brows and nodded.

Jessica raised her heavy beer mug to Becca. Becca clanked it with hers. They both drew long tastes of the brew, wishing for better things to come. Well, at least Becca did.

*B*ecca lugged the designer suitcase—the one that took her almost a week's salary to buy— into her bedroom and swung it up onto the bed. She took in a deep breath and then blew it out, pushing away the strands of hair that fell into her eyes. Her eyes darted to the open closet where she viewed her clothes. As she crossed over to the closet, she thought about the things she'd toss into the suitcase. It was October, so the days could be warm with tad cooler nights. Unfortunately, she didn't own a single pair of jeans. She tossed in her slim fitting designer slacks, a couple of blouses, and matching silk scarves for good measure. Next, she needed to pick out shoes.

After she had packed the essentials, it was time to go over her itinerary. Her flight was departing JFK Airport at 10:00 AM and would be arriving at Dallas/Fort Worth

Airport five hours later, where she'd pick up a rental car and drive another two hours to Steam. She scanned her phone for her hotel reservations. When she was satisfied that everything was in order, she settled in for the evening, curled up with her Kindle and a cup of chamomile tea.

EXCLUDING A SMALL AMOUNT OF TURBULENCE, the flight was uneventful. Becca picked up her sporty red Corvette, and other than one stop to use the bathroom and get a latte, she drove straight to Steam. She was pretty excited about this assignment, and the sooner she arrived in Steam, the sooner she could leave and get her shopping done in Dallas.

Becca had been a reporter for the specialty magazine featuring unsolved crimes for about three years. Her experience in covering stories went from writing about missing gnomes that showed up years later, to a missing teen who was reunited with her family. The most recent one was a person who'd been located after they went missing years ago and was now living a whole new life with no memory of the previous one.

She was thankful it was still daylight for her long drive. She'd never been to Texas before, and even though she was a tough broad from New York, her awareness of being a single, good-looking lady, driving by herself in a sporty car had her cognizant of her surroundings. She was an investigator, after all.

After driving the long and lonely roads that would lead her to Steam, she finally pulled into the parking lot of the town's one and only hotel. She spotted a small diner adjacent to the hotel. She lifted her suitcase out of the trunk and rolled it to the office. This hotel had a familiar look, but she wasn't quite sure … oh, the Bates Motel from that movie …

She checked in with the clerk who smiled and nodded a lot but didn't speak much. When he did, he talked with a slow drawl that reminded Becca she was in Texas.

She took her key and headed to her room. She glanced at her watch. No wonder she was hungry, it was past seven o'clock. She quickly checked to make sure no ax murderers were hiding in the closet, and then she headed out to find someplace for a bite to eat. Her appointment to meet Kyle Huntsman was in the morning.

BECCA ARRIVED at their designated meeting place ten minutes early. She found an empty booth and slid in. She ordered a cup of coffee and began to look over her notes when she noticed someone standing at the end of the table. Her eyes drifted up.

"Hi, you must be Rebecca Parsons from the magazine?"

Becca smiled at the handsome man dressed in a khaki uniform, sporting a shiny star prominently displayed on his shirt pocket. "Yes, I am. Kyle?"

The man pulled his hat off and then proceeded to slide into the empty side of the booth. "Yes, ma'am."

Becca straightened her back and lifted her shoulders slightly. She drew in a long breath and let it out as quietly as she could. He was strikingly handsome. These Texas boys were nothing to fool around with. "Please, call me Becca." She shifted her weight and clasped her hands in her lap. "I just ordered some coffee. Can I get something for you?" Becca asked as she twisted around, searching for the waitress.

"No, I'm good."

Becca focused on Kyle's dark brown eyes, noticing the golden flecks. Taken back by his handsome face she cleared her throat. "Thanks for meeting me. This is a very strange story, and I'm fascinated by it."

Kyle nodded. He pulled out some photos from his shirt pocket and laid them on the table. "This is a picture of my grandparents, Dirk and Lola Huntsman," he said.

Becca lowered her gaze to the pictures. "Are they still alive?" *Man, this guy sitting across from me is really cute.*

"Granddaddy just turned sixty-eight last week. Grandmother passed away last year."

"I'm sorry for your loss," she said as she jotted down

the information on the legal pad she'd brought with her. "What about your parents?" she asked.

"My dad, Robert Huntsman, is the sheriff here. My grandfather was the sheriff before him."

"I see. Your family has a long history of law enforcement. You're a sheriff, too?" She tipped her head toward the gold shield.

"Deputy. Pops is the Sheriff, but I'll take his place someday."

"Your mother …" Becca murmured.

"Gone, too. She had cancer," Robert said, lowering his gaze away from Becca's eyes.

Becca pulled her brows together. "All the women are gone? It's just you, your dad, and your grandfather?"

"Yep, three bachelors all living under the same roof." His eyes darkened, and Becca found it utterly sexy. She quickly looked away.

"What can you tell me about that day in 1956?"

"Well, let's see. Granddaddy was about seven years old. He'd been sent on an errand, and when he returned home, he found both his parents gone."

"That seems a bit young to be sent off to do an errand. Did he see anything unusual when he entered the house?" Becca asked, pausing as she took notes.

"That was a different time. Kids were sent out to get stuff all the time. At least that's what I've been told. And, no, he didn't really think anything about it at first. He thought maybe they were out back tending the garden.

The tea kettle was whistling on the stove and about out of water. The kitchen radio was playing, too."

"That's just odd." Becca chewed on her pen.

"It would be odd if you or I came upon it, but for a youngster, he just thought they got busy outside." He squared his shoulders and rapped the table with his fingers. "Listen, we're getting ready to have a big festival here for the celebration of fall and Halloween. Of course, every kid will bring up the story and add some stuff that didn't really happen."

"Like what?" She tilted her head.

"Oh, you know, typical dumb kid stuff. They were killed, and their bodies were buried under the house. Or they ran away because they didn't want my grandfather. But the best one is that they see their ghosts through the windows from time to time."

"So, the house is still standing?"

Kyle nodded. "It's just an old white clapboard farmhouse. The land is worth something. We just haven't been able to sell it."

"Okay, well, I'll mention that the land is available in my article. Maybe someone will see it and offer to buy it." She jotted down a note on her yellow legal pad. She laid the pen down and eased back in the booth. She felt really comfortable around this handsome deputy. "What's your take on what really happened?" She locked eyes with him and wondered if he really was single. She rarely took guys at their word regarding their marital status. She'd been burned before. She blinked a few times.

"The house is out in the country. Someone could have easily come by and kidnapped them. From what Granddaddy and Pops have told me, his parents loved him. He never felt anything but love. The theory that they up and left him is just plain ludicrous. There is another theory, though, and it might make more sense." He played with the rim of his hat while searching for his words.

Becca's eyes lifted from his strong hands when he caught her looking.

"Great-granddaddy was a gambler."

"So, maybe someone hurt them over an unpaid debt?" Becca chewed the inside of her cheek.

"Maybe. We'll never know. Anyone who had details about his gambling is long gone."

"So, tell me about the festival that takes place here every year."

"It's really a harvest festival. We celebrate fall and the bounty the earth provides. My great-grandparents had a huge farm and garden. They grew corn, onions, potatoes, and more."

"Okay, so you're not really celebrating the anniversary of their disappearance then."

"It was the day before Halloween when they disappeared. Granddaddy was sent to the store to get some sugar. His mother was going to bake some cookies. The one and only grocery store in town was about a twenty-minute walk from their house."

"So, in maybe about forty minutes this all took place?" She arched her brows as she scribbled something down.

"Well, not exactly. He stopped to play on the railroad tracks and lost track of time. Then these teens came out of nowhere and roughed him up."

"How old were these teens?"

"He thinks about seventeen or so."

"And he'd never seen them before?"

Kyle leaned back in the booth. "The police and the FBI have combed through this story a million times. You're not going to find anything new or different." He picked up the photos and stuck them back into his front shirt pocket.

"I didn't mean anything by it. I'm just curious, is all." She closed her notebook and tucked the pen in the spiral binding.

"I'm sorry. I didn't mean to snap at you." His eyes softened and made her feel less defensive.

"No worries. I'm just sorry your family didn't get any closure. It's really important in unsolved crimes, but I'm sure you know that." She picked up her purse and drew the strap over her head. "I'll come by during the festival and see all the fun before I head home." She slid out of the booth and stood, leaving some money on the table to cover her coffee and a tip.

"Let me walk you out."

She tipped her head and moved toward the door.

Kyle pushed open the door for her. She couldn't help but notice his strong muscular arms and calloused hands as he held the door for her. He smiled as she passed through. She smiled back.

"So, where did you say you were from?" he asked.

"New York. New York City, in fact."

"You're a big-city girl." He chuckled, digging his hands deep into his pockets.

Her eyes travelled the length of his long lean body. She couldn't help but notice how built he was, how handsome. And when he smiled, two dimples, one on his chin and one on his cheek, lit up his entire face.

"You could say that. I live on the fifteenth floor of a high-rise apartment building. I don't own a car. I take public transportation everywhere. And I eat a lot of take-out."

He smiled then he laughed. "But you drove here?"

"I keep my license current because of all the travelling I do for my job. But when I'm home, I take the subway or a taxi."

"I could never live in New York."

She pulled her chin up and narrowed her eyes. "Why not?"

"I like the easy living country life," he said with just a hint of a drawl.

"Well, I could never live out here," she playfully chimed.

"Why not?" he asked, frowning.

"Because of ... because ..." Her eyes widened and she smiled. "Because there are no sushi restaurants here."

"Sushi! You eat raw fish?" He laughed out loud.

It was ironic how she was out here in a cow patty of a town, talking to some young guy, no matter how cute he was, and they couldn't be any more opposite. She chuckled. "I guess neither one of us could trade places, then. I couldn't give up my sushi, and what was it you couldn't give up?" she said, mocking him.

"My truck," he said with a twang.

The two walked across the parking lot to her car. She had at least enough information to start the article. She hoped to get more of a feel for the town after the festival started.

"Here we are," he said.

She noticed he had parked his sheriff's car next to hers. She turned her body slightly toward him. "Thanks again for taking the time to meet with me. I think I have enough to get started on the story. When does the festival start?"

A large smile swept across his face. "Tomorrow, noontime, and it goes until Sunday evening."

"Okay, I'll probably see you around then. I'll definitely come out. I'd like to interview some townspeople candidly ... if that's alright?"

"Sure," he said. Then he gave her a little wink.

She felt herself begin to flush and was grateful for the cool breeze. She lowered her gaze. "Thanks again, Kyle." She had her hand on her door lever but hesitated opening it.

"Becca," he called.

She let go of the handle and smiled. She casually turned around. "Yes?"

"Would you like to go with me to the festival?"

Becca relaxed her shoulders. Not wanting to sound too eager she paused. "Sounds lovely. What time do you want to pick me up?"

She hesitated briefly before getting into her car. She watched as he drove off, kicking up some gravel as he sped away.

ONCE SHE RETURNED to her hotel room, she kicked off her shoes, and dropped down on the springy mattress. This big city girl got a taste of small-town charm, and she had to admit it, she kind of liked it. Wiping the smile off her face, Becca fired up her laptop, and while nibbling on some crackers she'd packed, she drafted her outline. She had the television on in the background, but wasn't really paying much attention until she heard the local news from the next town over. They made mention of the disappearance and of the festival. "That should add to the number of festival goers," she said out loud, shaking her head.

She finished her outline and then headed off to bed. She tossed and turned for a while as she revisited their conversation. Finally, her eyes got droopy, and she fell asleep.

CHAPTER 3

Refreshed and ready to take on the festival … and Kyle, Becca dressed in her black leggings, a silvery crew neck cashmere sweater, a silk scarf in soft grey, white, and just a dash of yellow, and her black ballet flats. As she waited for Kyle to pick her up, she worked on her draft. When she heard the soft knock on her door, she closed her laptop and rushed over to answer it.

"Good afternoon, Becca."

Grabbing her coat from a nearby chair, Becca crossed over to him where he waited in the doorway. "I'm ready for hayrides and bobbing for apples," she said, winking.

He let out a low chuckle, his eyes travelling up and down her body. "Wow, is this what girls from New York wear to country festivals?"

Becca shrugged her shoulders then lowered her gaze

to her black shoes, giving the toes a tap on the floor. "It's all I have." She lifted her eyes and stared at him.

"It's okay. I just don't want to ruin your fancy clothes, is all."

"It wouldn't be the first time something of mine got ruined." She lifted her brows when she thought of Jack and the spilled coffee.

"Well, then let's head on out." Kyle motioned for her to take the lead. "After you," he said.

Becca exited the hotel and wandered over to the passenger side of the car. She'd just reached out and placed her hand on the door lever when he quickly jogged around her to open the door, placing his hand on top of hers. Her eyes locked with his dark brown eyes momentarily. Her gaze dropped to his rugged, square jawline, then his mouth and finally his chin, where a cute dimple dared her to touch it. She swallowed hard, and slowly slid her hand out from under his and took a step back. Kyle opened the door for her and she slid in letting out the breath she hadn't even realized she'd been holding. Shaken from this exchange of sexiness and awkwardness, rolled into one iconic episode, Becca tried to clear her head. "Stay focused on the story, Becca," she said under her breath.

The quick drive into town soon had them parked and walking around the festival. The two walked quietly, weaving in and out of all the festival goers. Becca smiled and nodded at the friendly townspeople, whose broad smiles made her feel like a girl on a date. Kyle's down-to-earth personality, along with his handsome ruggedness, had her feeling a bit off-balance. She didn't typically go for the easygoing, laid-back kind of guy. Her men were usually loud, obnoxious … and loaded with money. Kyle was different … so very different. Her eyes lit up when they came upon the cotton candy booth.

Kyle held up a finger to the guy behind the counter and ordered one cotton candy.

"A very large crowd showed up today," Becca said, nodding forward as she nibbled on the sugary treat.

Kyle motioned toward an open space where a bench came into view. "Let's sit for a while."

Becca continued to devour the cotton candy he had treated her to. "Do you ever find yourself bored living in a small town?" She couldn't help but focus on the cute little lines around his eyes and face, probably from squinting in the sun, or the dimple on his left cheek. Suddenly she found herself fantasizing about planting a soft kiss first on the dimple on his cheek and then on that dimple squarely in the middle of his chin. Absently, she took another bite of the pink sugary delight.

"*Hmm*, not really." His eyes glistened in the sunlight. "If I want a taste of the big city, I drive to Dallas. After a weekend there, I remember why I love Steam so much." He tipped his hat off his head and swiped his forehead.

Just then, an older couple walked by and nodded.

Kyle waved and smiled in return. "I guess everyone in this town knows you." Becca kicked a pebble in the dirt.

"I guess you could say that." He laughed.

Their eyes locked for a moment then he leaned forward his fingers getting very close to her face. So much so she pulled back slightly.

"You have a little something," he said flicking a piece of the fluffy candy off her face, "on your face." A warm smile pulled up on the corners of his mouth.

"I'd like to meet your granddaddy … *um*, if that's okay?" she said, stumbling a bit over her words.

"Pops and Granddaddy love visitors. I'll set it up."

Becca crossed her legs at the ankles and smiled. "I bet you're good at shooting." She tipped her head toward the festival booth with milk bottles lined up.

"I've been known to hit a few," he said, his eyes doing that twinkling thing again, quickening Becca's pulse.

She uncrossed her legs and jumped up. Grabbing his hand, her heart hammered in her chest like a young girl on a first date, as she led him to the shooting gallery He paid for the game, selected a gun, and took aim.

"*Pop, pop, pop,*" the gun sounded, as he shot down one bottle after another.

A couple of the bottles sprang back up.

"This game is rigged," he whispered in her ear, leaning in and causing the hair on the back of her neck to crawl.

After a few moments, the booth owner walked over

with two stuffed animals. A broad smile formed on her face as she pointed to the brown horse with a yarn mane. "I've gotta keep in the theme of Texas … cowboys, and all." She winked.

"You don't think we have pandas here in Texas?" His forehead crinkled as he snickered.

She gazed at his plump lips and then moved her eyes upward. Drawing in her bottom lip, she looked this fine man over, and sighed. "You win."

She knew she could have answered him back with, "In the zoo," but she let it go. She'd learned a long time ago to only go after the battles worth fighting. This wasn't one of them.

CHAPTER 4

"How'd things go with that New Yorker journalist?" Kyle's Granddaddy Dirk asked as he shuffled into the kitchen.

"Went well. She wants to meet you and Pops. I was thinking we could have her over for supper." Kyle pulled a cup down from the cabinet and handed it to his granddaddy.

Dirk's eyes widened as he poured his coffee.

"I mean, she's very nice and she came all this way." Kyle tilted his head toward him.

"Okay. What does your dad think about all of this?" He elevated his brows and waited.

"I haven't run it by him yet."

"Good morning," Robert Huntsman bellowed as he came around the corner.

Kyle whiffed the air as his dad rushed to the cabinet for a cup.

"Boy, I can smell the Old Spice this morning, Pops. Who are you trying to impress?" He winked at his granddaddy and then turned his attention back to his dad.

Robert wrinkled his forehead. "No one. I guess I just got a bit heavy-handed with the stuff." He poured the stout, black coffee into his cup and drew it to his lips, blowing on it first.

"You sure? 'Cuz I heard that Ms. Lilly is in town." Kyle laughed.

"Boy, mind your own business. By the way, how did it go with that fancy New York journalist? Will they ever just leave us alone?" He pulled out a chair at the wooden, butcher block style farmhouse table and sat down.

"Becca? She's very nice. I was just telling Granddaddy that I'd like to have her over for dinner. She would like to meet you both."

Robert guffawed. "Since when do we have to entertain journalists?"

"Not entertain—visit with. She's really nice. I had a great time with her at the festival. She's not at all what I expected."

"You mean, snobby and self-absorbed?" Dirk asked.

"Pops!" Kyle said.

Robert and Dirk laughed loudly.

"I'd say someone is a bit sweet on a certain journalist," Dirk said, winking toward Robert.

Kyle decided it was better to just let things go. Otherwise this teasing could go on for hours. Instead, he smiled, and to show them he could take all the ribbing they could dish out, he popped them a salute before heading toward the hallway.

"I HOPE my lasagna will be good enough for her. I'm sure she's used to eating at some really fine restaurants." Dirk peered inside the oven at the bubbling red sauce in the pasta dish.

"She'll love it, Granddaddy. And she'll be impressed that an almost seventy-year-old can still work his magic in the kitchen."

"The Huntsman men are not wimps. We know how to take care of ourselves."

Kyle patted his granddaddy on the shoulder. "I'm going to go get her. I'll be back soon."

Just as Kyle passed through to the other room, Robert came in from the hallway. "Going to go get Ms. High Society?" He bowed his brows.

Kyle vehemently shook his head. "You'll see. She's not like that at all."

"I HOPE I LOOK ALRIGHT?" Becca's eyes travelled to her

feet and then back up her cream double-woven knit pants.

"You look great. We're very informal at the Huntsman house."

She slipped her fingers inside her waistband and gently tucked down her chiffon, button-down blouse. "I better expand my wardrobe to include blue jeans and peasant tops if I get any more assignments in small towns." A warm smile crossed her face.

"Well, I bet you will look just as good in your blue jeans as you do in your designer clothes."

Standing openmouthed she said, "So, you do know these are designer clothes?"

Squaring his shoulders, he lifted his chin in a grander way. "Sure. I may live out in the sticks, but I know expensive stuff when I see it."

"So, it is out of place then?" Her shoulders slumped.

"Listen, as long as you are the same person I had fun with at the festival, it doesn't matter what you're wearing. Just be yourself. Clothes do not make the person." He put his arm around her and moved her forward toward the car. "Granddaddy made his specialty for you." Kyle opened the door of the sheriff's car and motioned for her to climb in.

"I promise not to drill your family for details. That's not why I'm here. They send us out on stories all the time to see if any new developments have arisen in an unsolved case." She studied his profile.

"That's fine. As I told you the other day, we love visitors, and I don't really mind retelling the story. I guess Granddaddy might, but he knows it's sort of what put Steam on the map, so it goes with the territory."

It'd been a while since he'd let any girl ride in his car, let alone the official car of Steam, but something about Ms. Becca stirred him up. Maybe it was her baby blue eyes, or the way she giggled at his not so funny jokes, or maybe it was the mere fact that he couldn't have her that drove him wild with curiosity. He drew in a deep breath and brought with it the scent of lavender and hints of vanilla and sandalwood.

THEY DROVE for a while before Kyle pulled onto a long dirt and gravel road. A white farmhouse appeared and he stopped in front of it. "Here we are." He cut off the engine and grabbed the keys.

They exited the car, walked to the house, and started up the steps. Taking the last two steps at once, Kyle reached the screen door and opened it. "After you," he said, tipping his head.

"Something smells delicious," she said following him deeper into the house.

As they passed through a cozy living room furnished with overstuffed chairs and a well-worn sofa covered in a thick Sherpa throw, a large dog greeted them.

"That there is Duke," he said, motioning to the black and tan eighty-pound German shepherd.

She gingerly patted his head.

Kyle threw his head back and laughed. "He doesn't bite."

"I'm just not used to being around police dogs." She winced.

"Old Duke isn't a police dog, he wouldn't hurt a flea. Would you, boy? So you never had any pets?"

She shook her head.

"Not even a goldfish?" He arched his left brow and waited.

She shook her head once again.

Kyle turned his attention away from Duke and focused on the man sitting in the recliner. "Pops, this is Becca. Becca, this is my dad, Robert."

Robert jumped from his seat and made his way over to her with his hand extended. "It's nice to meet you. Hope you've found the folks of Steam hospitable."

A grunt came from around the wall and out came Dirk, holding a dish towel.

"Granddaddy, this is Becca," Kyle said, pointing toward her.

"I gathered that, boy." He wiped his hands on the towel and walked over to her, extending one for a handshake. "Dirk Huntsman," he introduced himself.

"Rebecca Parsons, but my friends call me Becca."

"Dinner will be ready shortly. Would you care for a glass of wine?"

"Sounds good," she murmured.

"Have a seat. We don't do fancy around here, but Granddaddy loves a good glass of wine."

"Kyle tells me you've never been to Texas before. What do you think?" Robert focused on her eyes.

"I like it. It's a bit dusty out here, but I guess you get used to it." She crossed her feet at the ankles and clasped her hands on the table.

"Here's a Zin that Granddaddy swears will put hair on your chest." Kyle handed her a wineglass.

"Well, I hope it doesn't do that," Becca said, drawing a taste of the red juice.

Kyle spun around when he heard his granddaddy using a few choice words. "Excuse me." He rushed to help Granddaddy take out the glass casserole dish.

"Thanks, boy. It was a bit heavier than I remembered it being." He laughed.

"It's from the ton of cheese you use." Kyle placed the casserole dish on a trivet before making his way back to the table where he braced his hands on the chair back and listened. "Dinner is cooling." He nodded.

"So, you're a big-city girl, *huh*?" Robert asked.

"I guess you could say that. I was born outside of the city but moved to New York City after high school." She looked around Robert and watched as Kyle helped in the kitchen.

"Dinner is ready," Kyle said, placing four different bottles of salad dressing squarely in the middle of the table. Grab your plate and help yourself to the lasagna.

Becca went first and Granddaddy served up a nice slice. He then motioned for her to take a slice of bread from the foil packet. With her full plate, she headed back to the table and sat down.

Twisting his head to get Kyle's attention in the kitchen, Robert yelled out, "Kyle, fetch the croutons."

Kyle opened a cabinet and brought out a can of store-bought croutons and set it on the table.

"This stuff is pretty good on salads," he said, smiling.

Becca lifted her shoulders to her ears as a puzzled look appeared on her face. "Great," she said, tipping her head. She sat across from Kyle, while Robert and Dirk sat at each end of the table. "This lasagna is delicious," she said, smiling at Dirk.

"Thank you, hon."

They chatted about the festival, and Robert mentioned they had a drunk in the cell sleeping off too much alcohol.

Becca put her fork down and tasted her wine again. "I guess it can get pretty lonely out here. Is drinking an issue for the residents?"

Kyle creased his brows. "No. He was just having fun and overindulged."

"What do you do for fun around here?" She figured she'd change the subject.

"Ride horses, go to the movies … yes, we have a theater … hang out on the front porch and listen to the night owls and watch the fireflies." His eyes twinkled, and then he picked up his wine glass. "I love it out here." He took a sip.

"Now, tell us what it is you like about New York City," Robert said.

"I love the nightlife, the restaurants, and … shopping," she said with a sheepish grin.

"Have you ever been robbed?" Granddaddy asked.

Becca shook her head. "No! I try to always be in a group, and I have my pepper spray handy at all times." She giggled.

"Well, here you don't have to worry about any of that, and if some creep did bother you, you'd just introduce him to your buddy Smith & Wesson."

The three men almost fell out of their chairs laughing so hard.

"How about some dessert?" Granddaddy leaped from his chair.

"Cheesecake on behalf of the grocery store." He sliced up the dessert placing pieces on plates.

"Let's go out on the front porch so Becca can hear the cicadas." Robert led the way, armed with his pie.

Rocking chairs lined the porch, and Kyle let her know which one she could sit in. "Granddaddy's and Pops'," he said, motioning to the first two.

She plopped into the third chair and began rocking as

she took small bites of the cold, creamy dessert. Suddenly, she saw little lights flashing out in the distance. "Fireflies," she said in admiration.

"Yep, every night during the summer and early fall you can find them playing and chasing one another, right here from the porch." Kyle drew in a deep breath. It was unusually warm, but the mugginess of summer in the south wasn't there, and the fresh night air felt good in his lungs and on his body. He wondered if it felt as good to Becca.

"Dirk?" Becca said.

"*Uh-huh*," he said in a low drawl.

"Wondered if I could ask you a few questions?"

"Sure."

"Do you think those teens you met on the track that day may have had something to do with your parents' disappearance?"

"I have no earthly idea. Maybe, but it most likely was just a coincidence they were there that day. I don't see how two punk teens could have taken my Pa down, or my mother, for that matter."

She sighed and then went back to rocking and watching the fireflies flit around.

"Granddaddy said he didn't see any weapons on them, but that doesn't mean they couldn't have hidden them in the brush near the tracks," Kyle said.

Becca raised her brows. "Sure, that makes total sense, Kyle.,"

Through half closed lids, Kyle studied her face. Even in the darkness of night, he could see how beautiful she was, and the thoughts that ran through his mind were downright naughty.

"Anyway, it's an unsolved case and always will be. But as long as there are journalists out there who need a story to write about, we'll never be able to forget about that day," Robert said soberly.

"I'm sorry. I feel bad for being the one to bring it up, but it's why I'm here, Becca explained.

"No worries. I'm glad you came. I would have never met you, otherwise," Kyle said, flashing a wide grin. He wanted to say more, but the timing wasn't right.

She shook her head. "Thanks for understanding. I'm never really sure how I'll be accepted when I come out on one of these assignments."

After that, the only sounds for some time were that of the old wooden chairs rocking in rhythm on the old front porch.

"I'll take you home when you're ready." Kyle interrupted the silence.

"I probably should be going. I have an afternoon flight, so I need to get up and get going after breakfast." She stood and stretched. "It was nice meeting you all. Thanks again for the hospitality." She nodded to both Robert and Dirk.

"Come back anytime." Dirk winked at Kyle.

The two made their way to Kyle's truck. He opened

the door for her and like the gentleman he was raised to be, he offered his hand to her as she stepped up into the cab. He made sure she was settled before shutting the door. He skipped around the front of the truck, running his hand along the hood as he made his way over to the driver's side. He jumped in, started the motor, and soon they were travelling down the gravel driveway that led to the main road.

After a few moments of silence, Kyle spoke. "Granddaddy is funny, right?"

"What do you mean?" She didn't take her eyes from the side window.

"Oh, never mind," he said, figuring she didn't see his wink. *I wonder what she'd do if I reached out and placed my hand on her leg.*

He wouldn't find out because they had reached the hotel.

"Don't take this wrong, but don't you ever just long to live in a city? For the bright lights, noise, and hotel brands that are known worldwide?" She tipped her head toward the hotel.

"Not for a second. I like the easy living of this small town. Even with our scary looking hotels," he said, laughing.

"So, you know what I mean about the hotel?" Her eyes widened as she circled the car and drew nearer to him.

"Yes. We used to make reference to that movie and

this hotel when we were teenagers," he said walking her to the door.

"Thanks again for everything," she said.

"Well, I guess you better get inside and write up your report. I gave you my email at the office. Just shoot it to me when it's ready. I'm sure you'll write a good story." He smiled.

She slipped the key into the lock and gave it a twist. She turned with her back up against the door and grinned. "I had a great time. Your family was so nice, despite me being from New York. They really rolled out the red carpet."

He reached out and cupped her hands with his. A breeze blew by at the same moment and brought with it a hint of her perfume. His heart hammered in his chest.

"So … I know you live in New York and all, but if you ever find your way back here again, would you stop in and visit?" He squeezed her hands.

She nodded. "Sure, but what business would I have that would bring me back to Steam?"

Okay, was this bait or was this thing he felt between them only one-sided. No way! She had to feel the same quickening pulse, the sweaty palms, the dry mouth. He pulled her in and kissed her.

Her eyes widened momentarily like saucers, and then she relaxed letting out a long breath. "I didn't see that coming."

"I'm sorry. I probably shouldn't have done that. It's just …"

She took his hands and slid them around her waist. "No, I'm glad you did." Her hands slipped up his chest and she wrapped her arms around his neck, playing with the hair that hung just below the nape. "I've wanted to kiss you for a while."

"You did?" He pulled back, rocking her gently, staring into her baby blues sparkling eyes.

"You had me when you smiled and those dimples popped up. I was like … yeah, super sexy." She winked.

He pulled her close and kissed her neck, trailing the kisses back to her mouth. She softly groaned, but halted the kiss.

"Yeah, I better get in and write up that report." She reached back opening the door behind and stepping inside. "Let's meet for coffee tomorrow before I head out? I'll have the rough draft completed, and if you give it your approval, I can go ahead and forward it to my chief editor."

"Okay, sounds great. Let's meet at the diner at around seven o'clock. Good night," he said, walking backwards..

Becca waved goodbye and closed the door.

He slumped against the closed car door, breathing heavily, and trying to calm his racing heart. *What the heck just happened?*

CHAPTER 5

She got to the diner before him. It had been a restless night after their impulsive kiss. She closed her eyes thinking about his soft lips and those dimples. A waitress interrupted her daydream and she ordered coffee and began looking over her notes.

"Good morning," a booming voice said.

She looked up to see Kyle standing by her table. His wide smile and dancing brown eyes made it difficult to contain her happiness at seeing him. In her most cheerful tone she replied, "Good morning," And gesturing to the bench across from her. "Have a seat."

He slid into the booth and peered over his shoulder to get the attention of one of the servers.

Soon, a gum snapping bleached blonde was leaning over their booth. "Good morning, Kyle."

"Hey, Krisi. Black coffee, please."

Something familiar passed between them, and Becca tightly twisted her mouth and raised her brows as she watched their flirtatious exchange. These two clearly had a past. Or at least a one-night stand.

Kyle noticed her pinched expression as soon as Krisi left, and leaned over the table. "We used to date a long time ago. Nothing going on there." He grinned mischievously. "You're not jealous, are you?"

She crossed her legs, bumping the table underneath. "Ouch." She quickly uncrossed them. "No. Jealous? Not in the least. Why should I be?" She drew in a taste of her coffee.

"Here you go, sweetie," Krisi said, dropping off his coffee. "Are you going to order breakfast?" She snapped her gum again, irritating Becca to no end. How rude!

"Nothing for me," Becca said.

"Just the coffee, Krisi. Thanks, hon."

Krisi swept her hand across his shoulder as she walked away.

"Do you call all your old girlfriends hon?"

"Whoa, I do believe Ms. New York is jealous."

Becca slid over the paper she'd printed out on the hotel's printer. "I was shocked to find out the hotel had a printer. And the desk clerk was creepy." She folded her hands.

"Oh, Jeffrey? He's harmless."

She leaned back against the tufted booth and sighed. "Let me know what you think."

He dropped his eyes to the document and began to read. When he got to the end he flipped it over. "This is it?"

A half smile crossed her mouth. She folded her hands neatly on the table and nodded.

He cleared his throat and then tossed the paper aside. "You call this good journalism?" His stare caused her to fidget.

"What don't you like about it?" she managed to squeak out.

"I take objection to a lot that is in here." He picked the sheet back up and scanned it.

"What objections do you have? I thought I was fair in my reporting." She sat back in the booth with slumped shoulders.

"The first thing is your suggestion that my grand-daddy might have been able to change what happened that day, had he not lingered on the tracks. How dare you make him feel guilty for that?"

"I just meant that if he wasn't sent out on the errand, maybe it wouldn't have happened." She lowered her head and stared at the table.

"That's not how this reads," he said, jabbing his finger at a section and rattling the paper, startling her.

Becca shifted her weight. "I don't mean any disrespect to you or your family. It's just a rough draft. That's why I'm sharing it with you today. I want to write something you'll be proud of, that Steam will be proud of."

"Well, you'll have to do a complete rewrite if you want to make us proud. It's bad enough Granddaddy has to live with the what-ifs. You don't have to put it in print. And the rumors already run rampant here, especially during fall festival time. So, yes, if you want to make yourself appear like a stand-up sort of gal, you'll fix all of this and submit it again for my approval." He slid out of the booth and stood with his arms crossed.

She pulled her purse from beside her and crossed the strap over her head, and then gathered the rest of her things and exited the booth. "I'm sorry for the misunderstanding, Kyle."

He uncrossed his arms and retrieved his wallet, tossing some bills on the table.

She suddenly felt like a total heel for upsetting him and for writing a crappy copy. She found his love for his family really endearing, and at that moment, all she really wanted to do was wrap her arms around him and tell him how sorry she was. But instead, she walked away. Saying sorry was never one of her strong suits.

"OKAY, TELL ME AGAIN ABOUT KYLE," Jessica said, leaning back in her swivel office chair.

"He's gorgeous. He has these dancing brown eyes with yellow flecks, a dimple on his chin and one on his cheek that I just wanted to kiss all day long, and he's just dreamy all the way around. We had a great time together until the morning I left. He read the article rough draft and flew off the handle."

"Let me read it." She leaned forward and held out her hand.

Becca scanned the stack of papers on her desk and then retrieved one, handing it to her.

Jessica gasped. "Well, this isn't really reading very friendly." She peered over the top of the paper.

"Oh, please, not you, too."

"Well …" She grimaced.

"I know, let me guess. It's not sugary enough. Soft enough." The words flew out of her mouth in an angry tone. "It's a draft, for Pete's sake. A D-R-A-F-T …"

"Okay, fair enough. But how long have you been a journalist? You don't give someone a copy unless it's pretty much ready to go. Did that kiss he gave you fry your brain?" Jessica knitted her brows.

Becca grabbed the paper out of her friend's hands and leaned back. She scanned the document and then folded it in half and tossed it on her desk. "You're right. It's a piece of garbage. I don't know what I did there. It's definitely not my best work, and I'm sorry I didn't proof-read better before handing it to him. I was just so excited to see him." She lowered her head.

"Okay, this can be rectified. You fix that up," Jessica said, nodding toward the paper. "Give it to me to read, and then you'll email it to him with an apology. Reiterate that you haven't been a paid journalist for very long. That should soften his stance, and then you can finish the email with a formal apology along with the uploaded revision."

"No."

"No?" Jessica stood. "I thought you wanted to fix this."

"I do. I'm going to do everything you said but one thing."

Jessica leaned her head slightly to the left.

"I'm going to hand deliver this bad boy." She pulled her chair in toward the desk and focused on her laptop.

The office had six desks, and every journalist sat busily working. The muffled sounds of employees talking on the phones or with colleagues across the desks, along with the sounds of keyboards clicking away, gave off a familiar rhythm for Becca to complete her story.

Soon, lights dimmed, and the only noise in the office came from Becca plucking out the last few words on her keyboard.

"Come on, Becca. I'm starving," Jessica said as she hovered over her. Like many evenings, Jessica and Becca had decided to grab a bite to eat after work.

Becca bit down on her bottom lip. "Just one more second," she said absently. "Done!" A big smile crossed her face as she pushed back her chair.

Becca reached up and switched off the remaining

lights, and the two friends walked outside. Jessica hailed a cab and they got inside. As two single young ladies living in the heart of all the action, they had their pick of any restaurant.

"Sushi?" Becca asked as she turned her attention from staring out the window to Jessica.

"Sounds great."

Becca leaned forward in the seat. "East 78th Street," she told the driver.

As she held a copy of Becca's story in one hand, Jessica grabbed a piece of roll with her chopsticks and plopped it into her mouth. Becca took a piece of roll for herself and watched Jessica as she chewed and read.

"Well?" she asked, while finishing her bite.

"This reads well. I think it conveys the apology perfectly. It's groveling at its best." She dropped the paper on the table and pushed it toward Becca.

"I hope so." Becca sipped some of her hot tea. "I really messed up with Kyle."

Jessica nodded. "But you know those country boys. They were brought up to accept apologies, especially from pretty fillies." Jessica laughed at her own joke.

Becca leaned forward. "I don't know what it is, but I really like him. I know we can't be together. Hell, he's in Texas. Dust Bowl, Texas, at that. I could never give up

New York, and he already told me he'd never be able to live in New York." She moved her plate and placed her elbows on the table, while cupping her face. "I think I'm fantasizing about something I could never have."

Jessica leaned forward to meet Becca half way. "Well, you could, *you know* … and just see if it's worth the risk." Her eyes grew big.

"Jessica! Are you suggesting I try out the merchandise?"

"Hey, every horse rides differently." She leaned back and crossed her arms, a smirk forming on her mouth.

The corners of Becca's lips curled. "There you go with the horse euphemism again."

THIS TIME she'd be prepared for her visit to Steam, Texas. She'd show him she could be more than a pretty face dressed in designer clothes. Becca pulled on the faded blue jeans and turned one way then another as she viewed herself in the dressing room mirror. She twisted her mouth as her eyes rested on the folded cuffs of the boyfriend jeans. "Maybe," she said, taking them off and pulling the next pair off the hanger to try on.

She studied the look of the full-length jeans with the slightly flared leg. "This probably would go good with boots," she said, as she recalled seeing some women wearing similar jeans at the festival.

The last pair she tried on, black with straight-leg, made her eyes light up. "Ooh, I really like these," she said as she unbuttoned them and tossed them in the pile.

Next, she moved to the casual tops, settling on T-shirts that matched her jeans. Happy with her purchases, she headed to the shoe department.

"I don't typically wear boots," she told the store clerk. "But I've been invited out to the country," she added, telling him a little lie.

"No worries," the young man said as he measured her foot. "I'll grab a few things that you might like." He jumped up from the stool and headed out to the floor.

Becca watched as he carefully considered each pair. He'd stand back, rub his chin, and then lean forward and pick up the shoes. He came back with four boxes stacked to his chin.

Becca began to quickly open each box. "I sort of like these."

"They look cute with straight-leg jeans. They come in lots of colors, too. This is our navy blue, but depending on what color your pants are, maybe the black, or even the khaki, would work."

"I'm looking for *easy to walk around on dirt roads in boots*, that sort of thing."

"Your best bet is the lightweight sneakers. They're very popular. You can't go wrong."

"Okay, I'll take the navy blue pair and a black pair as well. But I think I want to try on some cowboy boots, too." She straightened her shoulders, and raising her chin, she peered across the room to where the boots were displayed.

"I'll get your sneakers and grab a pair of boots for you to try on."

Becca admired the sneakers she'd chosen. She wore white sneakers when she played tennis, but other than that, she wore heels or ballet flats in a variety of colors. Becca looked up as the clerk headed her way with two pairs of boots.

"So, these look cute with skinny jeans and T-shirts," the clerk said, handing her an ankle boot. "I know you said you had ankle boots, but these have the cowboy heel." He smiled as he crossed his arms.

"These are super cute. So, these pass as real honest-to-goodness cowboy boots?" She arched her brows.

"Yep, they have the round toe and cowboy heel, and the leather laced design along the collar, and V-cut side make them chic and cute. As I said, great with skinny jeans."

"Let me try them on."

While the clerk went to get her size, Becca checked her phone for messages, just in case Kyle tried to call. Who was she fooling? He wasn't going to call. She tossed her phone back in her purse and sank deep into the chair. Soon the clerk produced her boots.

"I really like these," she said, modeling in the shoe mirror.

"You have small feet so the boots look just perfect."

Becca paid for her purchases and headed outside to hail a cab to take her home. Shopping always exhausted her.

While she looked out the taxi's window, she observed the cars lined up bumper-to-bumper as they crawled down the main avenue. The occasional honk or squeal of brakes reminded her all too well that she was back in New York City. She shook her head. When had she realized that being in such a hurry all the time was quite annoying? A small smile made its way across her mouth. When she had stepped foot onto the dusty roads of Steam, that's when. All of a sudden, the taxi driver slammed the brakes and all her packages went flying down onto the floorboard. She leaned over, retrieving her bags and placing them alongside her on the seat. He mumbled an apology of sorts and then proceeded with his stop-and-go erratic driving all the way to her apartment building. Happy to have both feet on the ground, Becca paid the driver and then proceeded to enter her building.

SHE SAT AT HER DESK, wringing her hands, trying to gather the courage to go in and see Jack Porter. She'd already heard through the gossip mill that he was questioning her return trip to Steam. She'd rehearsed what she was going to say to him. It was part of the journalist's pledge—stay until you get the story, or something like that. She drew in a deep breath and sighed. She pushed back her chair, nodded to Jessica, and then holding her head high, she almost raced to his office before she lost her courage and her motivation. She knocked once, waited for his greeting, and then entered his office.

"Becca," he said, nodding toward one of his guest chairs.

"I'll just be a minute." She nervously sat on the edge of the nearest chair.

"I hear you're heading back to Steam. Didn't you just come back from there?" Jack eyed her warily.

Becca swallowed down the lump in her throat. "Yes. Yes, I did. I need to go back, though."

"To finish the story?" He leaned back and a smirk settled across his face.

"No … well, yes … sort of. See, he didn't like the way I was going to write up the story. We were getting along just fine and then *WHAM!* He went ape crazy on me, and I can't leave it that way." Becca slumped down in her chair.

"Wait a second." Jack shook his head, trying to make sense of her blurted reasoning.

Becca leaned forward. "Kyle was upset with me. I can't leave it like that. I must go back to Steam and let him read the revision of the story. His family was so nice to me." A tear bobbled around on her lower lid.

"Okay, so you want to go back and make amends. I

like that. We want our stories to be truthful, and we always want people to think our work is honorable, as well as our employees. I'm granting you a few days to go finish that story." He pushed his chair back and stood.

Becca's jaw dropped, but she recovered quickly, stood, and extended her hand. "Thanks, Jack. I really appreciate it."

"No worries. Just come back." He smiled, shaking her hand.

"Is it that obvious?"

"Just a tad." He moved around the desk and opened the door.

"I don't usually fall for guys who I'm interviewing."

"And I imagine you don't usually tell your bosses that, either." He tilted his head and tightly pulled his mouth in. His eyes twinkled, though, letting her know he wasn't upset with her.

"I promise when I get back it will be balls to the wall."

Jack tossed his head back and laughed. "Okay, Becca. Go to Steam and tell your cowboy you're sorry. Then head on back home."

"I know we don't know each other very well. Seems I was gone when you came on board, and then I was off again. And then there's the little coffee incident. But I promise you that when I come back you'll get one hundred and fifty percent out of me."

Jack tapped her shoulder. "I know your work ethic. I know everyone's. That's what bosses do. I'm quite sure you'll prove to me that your work is impeccable. Take those few days of personal time and get things in order. We'll be right here when you get back."

Becca thanked him for his understanding. Happy it went so smoothly, she sashayed back to her desk, smiling ear to ear.

"I guess things went well?" Jessica smiled, folded her arms, and leaned back in her chair.

"You could say that." Becca returned the smile.

BECCA CHECKED into the same hotel she'd stayed at on her first visit to Steam. The clerk remembered her, but she wasn't sure if that was a good thing or bad. After taking her things to her room, she headed to the diner where she ordered a chef salad and water for dinner. As she ate, she tried to get up the nerve to make a visit to the sheriff's office, but decided that after a long day of travelling, her surprise visit would have to wait until the morning. She finished her dinner, paid her tab, and spent the rest of the evening channel surfing, but it was hard to concentrate. Her mind always seemed to wander back to Kyle and his warm caring eyes.

THE NEXT MORNING, she didn't feel much like eating, so

after two cups of coffee, she headed to town. Her anxiety was getting the better of her. She needed to resolve all her questions, and if she were to be completely honest, they were not just about Kyle's great-grandparents' disappearance

HER EYES FLASHED to the stenciled "Sheriff's Office" on the window as she opened the old creaky door and stepped inside. Both Kyle and Robert sat at desks with their heads down.

Robert made eye contact with her first. "Well, I'll be. What brings you back so soon?"

Just then, Kyle looked up, giving Becca a cool stare, as he shoved back his chair and stood. "What are you doing here?" he asked somewhat sternly.

"I came to see you," she said hesitantly, twisting her hands nervously before gaining control of her emotions. She willed herself to relax and let her arms dangle at her sides.

He came around his desk, stopping directly in front of her. She could smell his cologne and the sight of his dimple sent a tingle down her spine. It was almost too much for her to handle. She wanted to pull him in, tell him what a fool she'd been, and kiss him.

"I wanted to see you. I couldn't let things go on the way they were." She stepped closer toward him.

He shook his head. "I think you made your feelings pretty clear."

"I'm stepping out for some coffee," Robert called out. "It was nice seeing you again, Becca."

Becca nodded but didn't take her eyes off of Kyle. "Yes, nice to see you, too," she muttered.

"Becca." His eyes smoldered, drawing her in .

"Kyle," she breathed.

"Did you rewrite the story?" His eyes remained locked with hers.

She tore her gaze from his and dug through her satchel for the article. "Read it for yourself," she said handing him the document.

He took the paper from her hands and began to read. She watched him expectantly until he finished. He cleared his throat and let his hands drop to his side. "Thank you."

She stepped closer. "I hated that you were upset with me. The kindness you and your family showed me made me realize you all deserved a great story. I really wasn't trying to be a snob or coldhearted. I guess some of us journalists could use a dose of humility and to realize that it's not always about getting the story."

His expression softened and he leaned in kissing her cheek first before finding her mouth. She stepped closer so she could feel more of him, and he slipped his hands around her waist as he continued to kiss her. Opening her mouth slightly, she invited him in for more. After a few heavenly moments he pulled back from the kiss, holding her hands in his. "I missed you."

"I missed you, too. It's crazy," she said, shaking her head. "We just met. I mean, what the heck?"

"I know. It's an unlikely union, for sure." He smiled.

"Maybe that's the attraction? We both know we're really not each other's type. Maybe we want to just test the waters?" She gave him a come-hither look.

"How long are you here for?" He narrowed his eyes.

"Just a couple of days."

He leaned in, and just before he kissed her again, said, "More than enough time."

She placed her hand on his chest to stop the kiss. He pulled back with a startled look on his face. "What?"

"Let's go somewhere more private."

A wicked smile played on his lips as he released her from his embrace. He quickly retrieved his hat from the coat-tree and ushered out the door, closing it behind him. "Wait a second," he said, pausing. He reopened the door, flipped the door sign to read "Out to Lunch," then closed the door again.

CHAPTER 7

When he walked out to the kitchen drying his hair with a towel he got the immediate sense he was being stared at. "What?" He opened the fridge and looked inside.

"Is there any hot water left?" Robert teased Kyle.

Kyle smirked not taking his eye off the fridge contents. Grabbing the carton of orange juice he turned around.

"Well? Are you going to tell us what's going on?" Robert leaned back in his chair.

"Yeah, your dad tells me a pretty little lady made a visit to the office today." Granddaddy laughed as he lifted the lid to something he was cooking on the stove.

"Okay, guys, stop ribbing me. Yes, Becca came back into town. She wanted to hand deliver her story on us."

He poured a glass of juice and crossed to the table to join Robert.

Robert picked up the daily newspaper, and began to rifle through it.

"Couldn't she just send it by mail?" Granddaddy asked.

Kyle ignored him as he texted on his phone.

Granddaddy dished up the stew and placed a bowl in front of his son and another in front of Kyle, leaving himself for last.

"Sure smells good," Kyle said, sticking his spoon into the thick gravy and meat dish.

"Why didn't you invite Becca over for dinner?" Robert asked, closing the paper and focusing on Kyle's eyes.

"Uh, well, uh …" he stammered.

"Out with it, boy," Granddaddy said, showing absolutely no patience.

"She's resting. We're going to go out later."

"Resting? Resting from what?" Granddaddy pressed further.

Kyle tightly locked his lips. "Come on, stop with the twenty questions. She's tired from her long trip."

Robert raised his brows and turned his attention to Granddaddy, just in time to see him wink.

After dinner, the three men cleared the table, and while Robert and Granddaddy washed and stacked, Kyle made his excuses to leave them with their chores so he could get ready. When he came out to the main living area, both his dad and his granddaddy were nowhere in sight. He glanced around then shrugged. He exited the house and started to take the steps down when he heard his granddaddy's voice.

"YOU KIDS BE CAREFUL," a voice called out from the porch.

Kyle squinted as he stared into the dark space. "Granddaddy?"

"Just getting some night air."

Kyle ascended the steps and sat in one of the rocking chairs near him. Duke plopped down beside him and rested his head on his paws. "It's a great night. Look at the sky. It's lit up like crazy."

The sounds of the old rocking chairs as they moved back and forth and the occasional buzzing sound from insects lulled the two men into silence.

Finally, Kyle spoke. "I really like Becca. I don't know how I feel about her going back to New York."

"Yeah, that's the kicker, Son. Maybe you two should really think about that before it gets any more serious?"

"Too late for that." Kyle looked over at his granddaddy.

Granddaddy took in a deep breath and let it out

slowly. "That's what I was afraid of." He rocked some more.

"Maybe she would consider moving here?"

Granddaddy stopped the chair from rocking and leaned forward. "You know those city types could never survive out here. It would never work, Kyle."

"What if I moved there?"

Granddaddy's eyes widened. He shook his head a few times. "You'd be like a fish out of water, but I know when the heart is full of love, people do crazy stuff."

"Do you think two people from such opposite places could really make a go of it?"

Granddaddy raked his hand through his greying hair. "I do. Granted I don't know too many around here where that may apply, but I've read about it in books."

Kyle looked out toward his truck and then turned back to face his granddaddy. "I guess I'd always hoped I'd meet someone really special and even a little different to keep things lively." He winked.

"Well, she's definitely that." Granddaddy laughed.

"Sometimes when we talk, I feel like I'm talking to this really complicated woman. But then, I look into those magnetic eyes, and I just see someone who is looking for acceptance and love."

"Is that because that's what you want to see?" Granddaddy arched his brow.

"Could be. But I still feel something special when I'm

with her. It's like this city girl is teaching me things I didn't know I was missing."

Granddaddy's eyes widened.

"Not those things, Granddaddy." Kyle snapped his head back and chuckled.

"Well, Son, I bet you're teaching her a few things, too."

Kyle cocked his head and looked at his granddaddy with narrowed eyes. "How so?"

"She's a city girl. You're a country boy. Figure it out."

Kyle stood. "Well, I told her I'd be there soon. I should be going." He stood to leave.

Granddaddy went back to rocking and Kyle headed to his car and drove away.

HE REACHED down to turn the volume up on the radio, taking his eyes off of the dark country road for just a second. When he looked up, all he saw was a ten-point buck staring at him right before they collided. He slammed on the brakes and veered the truck to the right, going off the shoulder and coming to a halt, barely missing a huge boulder. Steam poured from the crumpled hood, as Kyle stepped out of the truck. Dizziness swept over him, and he recalled hitting his head on the steering wheel. Something sticky rolled down the side of his face and he wiped his hand across his face. Blood covered his fingers. He reached into the truck, pulled out an old T-shirt, and wiped his forehead. The road was pitch-black and he couldn't see more than a few feet in front of him, So he crawled back into the cab and called his dad first and then Becca.

ROBERT AND DIRK pulled up behind Kyle's badly battered truck.

"Kyle," Robert yelled, reaching him quickly.

"I'm okay. Just a little bump on the head."

"The hell you are," Kyle's granddaddy blurted.

"The truck is more messed up than me."

"We're getting you to the hospital. Let's go," Robert said, corralling Kyle toward the other vehicle.

"What about my truck?" Kyle peered over his shoulder as his dad pushed him toward the car door.

"I'll call a tow truck. Get in." He motioned for him to get into the front seat.

They drove to the hospital in Warm Springs, the next town over. It was a small hospital with only ten beds, but it had all the equipment necessary for most emergencies. If the patient required more, then they would be transported by helicopter to Dallas/Fort Worth.

"I'm alright," Kyle said, waving off the nurse who went to work cleaning his wounds.

"You have a four-inch gash on your forehead, Deputy Huntsman," the nurse said, ignoring his complaints.

"Kyle, you might have some internal injuries. The truck is pretty messed up, not to mention the deer," Robert said, trying to conceal his concern.

Kyle pulled himself up in the hospital bed and winced. "Anyone hear from Becca?"

"She's out in the waiting room," Granddaddy answered.

Kyle motioned toward his granddaddy with his hand. "Thanks. Can you go get her?"

"Right now, only family can come back here," the nurse interjected.

Kyle mumbled something under his breath.

"Rules are rules," she sang.

"Just get the doc in here so I can go home," he pleaded.

"He's on the way."

"Calm down, Kyle. You could have been killed. This is serious business. We have to make sure you check out okay. Once the doc gives the order, you can come home." Robert placed a hand on Kyle's shoulder and gently squeezed.

Kyle sighed, giving in. "Okay, Pops."

Over the course of the next two hours, Kyle endured X-rays and some lab work. While he waited for the verdict, he watched some television from the ceiling mounted TV—anything to keep his mind off the pain he was feeling and off of Becca. He wasn't sure which was worse.

"Okay, Kyle," the doctor said, whisking into the sterile, all white and chrome room.

Kyle pulled up on his elbows. "What's going on?" A small smile curled up on his mouth.

"You have a cracked rib, and of course, that nasty gash on your head, but other than that, no other injuries. Now, we have to keep that wound clean so that infection doesn't set in, and well, the ribs … they're going to be sore for a bit. I'll prescribe you some pain medication, and we'll keep them wrapped up. But it looks like bed rest will be the true prescription today." The doctor scribbled something on the chart and hung it back on the hook. "Any questions?"

Kyle shook his head. "Nope. Sounds like I'll be out of commission for a while."

"You'll heal fast. A young guy built like you will be up in no time."

They wheeled him out to the waiting area where Robert, Dirk, and Becca sat. They all jumped up when they saw him, bringing a wide smile to his face. "I'm free. I can go home," he said playfully.

"I was so worried about you," Becca said, leaning in and whispering into his ear.

He wanted to pull her down and kiss her. "I'm okay."

"Doc says he'll be out of commission for a while,"

Dirk said, rocking back and forth on the balls of his feet while he focused on Becca.

"He also said that young guys built like me heal fast." Kyle raised his chin and stared up at Becca and then winked.

"Well, let's get you home so you can start recuperating," Robert said.

Kyle gingerly rose from the wheelchair and slowly walked to the sliding glass doors that led them outside.

"I'm parked right out here," Robert said, holding out his arm

Kyle laced his arm with his dad's and exited the hospital.

Robert climbed into the driver's seat, and Granddaddy slid into the back seat, leaving the passenger side for Kyle.

Kyle and Becca held hands and leaned up against the car, trying to find a moment of privacy, but soon realizing that wasn't possible with the two men in the car waiting.

"Listen, I had a lot of things I wanted to say to you tonight." He tilted his head slightly.

"I had some things to say, too," she whispered.

"Give me a couple of days. I'll be good as new."

She nodded. "I can only stay for a few more days."

Narrowing his eyes, he brushed his fingers through his hair as he stared out into the night. "I'll make it up to you. I promise."

He stepped toward the passenger door and leaned forward to grab the door handle and grunted.

"Kyle?" she said in alarm.

"Just a little pain. I'm going to be fine."

He settled into the seat and she closed the door for him. He kept his eyes on her until he couldn't see her anymore.

$\mathcal{B}$ecca made it back to her hotel after a visit to the grocery store in Warm Springs, where apparently, all the stores were located. She bought a bottle of wine, a corkscrew, and a bag of potato chips. Stress eating and drinking were in order tonight.

After she binge-watched some reruns of an old television show, ate half the bag of chips, and drank half the bottle of wine, she decided to call Jessica … nothing like being woken by a tipsy and carb-laden friend.

"Oh, Becca, I'm so sorry. But he's going to be okay, right?" Jessica quickly interrupted before Becca could fill her in more.

"Yes, doctors say he'll make a full recovery. But—"

"But what? Did you get a chance to go horseback riding?" Jessica had a one track mind and it began to wear thin on Becca.

"Jessica! I know what you're inferring. How about I just tell you that some things are best left unsaid?" If Becca's stern words didn't let her friend know to back off on the subject, her tone certainly did.

"When do you have to come back to work?"

"Day after tomorrow." Becca felt sad just from saying the words.

"At least it's enough time to talk, even if you don't get to *you know* …" Jessica laughed.

Becca sighed into the cell phone. "He's just too sexy for his own good. Even with wrapped ribs and a gash on his forehead, I had a hard time resisting those warm, inviting chocolate eyes and dimples."

"What are you going to say to him?"

"I don't really know, but he said he had some stuff he wanted to tell me. I guess I'll let him go first. Anyway, I just wanted to chat with you for a moment before I went to sleep. Is everything going okay at the office?"

"Yes, I'm leaving tomorrow for Alaska again. So, if you can't get hold of me, just leave a message."

"Will do. Thanks, Jessica. When you get back, let's paint the town red."

"Sounds good. I heard there is a new nightclub opening up not far from the office. Maybe we can grab some of our stuffed shirt co-workers and let our hair down?"

Becca wondered if Kyle would fit in at that nightclub. She pictured him in faded blue jeans, a button-down shirt tucked neatly into his pants, a brown leather belt with a shiny buckle, and his brown cowboy boots and matching hat. He'd be an eyeful for the girls out on the dance floor.

"Okay, Jessica. Talk to you later."

She snuggled deeper under the covers and pulled them up to just under her chin. The more she thought of Kyle and his rugged handsomeness, the more she became aroused. She shook her head to clear the naughty images that kept weaving in and out of her mind. Sleep soon consumed her, but the thoughts of Kyle kept coming, and coming, and coming.

BECCA WOKE REFRESHED and ready to start her day. She dressed in her new clothes and shoes and headed out to find some coffee. Even though this was her second visit to Steam, she hadn't really explored the town. So, after a light breakfast of juice, coffee, and buttered toast, she hit the sidewalks and checked out Steam. The first place she came across was an antique store. When she opened the door and entered the store, a bell rang. She let her eyes adjust to the dimly lit store and wrinkled her nose at the musty smell.

She'd just rounded a corner when she came face-to-face with a tall, slender man with dark rimmed glasses. "Can I help you with something?"

Startling her, she gasped. "Oh, no, not really. I'm just visiting and thought I'd check out the town."

"I know who you are. You're that fast-talking newspaper lady from New York," he said in a Texas drawl.

"Magazine. I'm a journalist with a magazine here to do the story about—"

"I know who you are," he said, turning away. "Let me know if you need help."

Becca watched as he circled the large glass topped counter and began to leaf through a magazine. She drew in a deep breath and approached the counter. "Listen, we haven't met properly. My name is Becca Parsons." She held out her hand.

He paused then took her hand. "Andy Taylor," he said with a quick shake and release.

"Nice to meet you. I really like your store. You have a lot of interesting things in here."

He looked up from his magazine. "*Uh-huh.*"

"Can you tell me what the oldest item you have in here is?" She put her journalism skills to work and kept probing.

He walked around the counter, brushing past her. She watched and then followed him to a table where a small leather-bound Bible lay. "This is the oldest thing in my store."

"May I?" She motioned toward the book.

"Just be careful with it. The pages are really thin."

Becca gently picked up the book and turned it over in

her hands. She opened the front cover and closed it quickly. "How much?"

"Well, I looked up the value on the internet, and it said a Bible such as this could fetch close to two hundred dollars if in great shape."

"Sold. I'll give you that right now."

Andy furrowed his brows. "Just like that? You're not even going to try and whittle my price down?"

Becca shook her head.

"Why, I never! I thought all you big-city folks were hard-core. I'm impressed."

"You do realize that this Bible belonged to the Huntsman family?" Becca asked.

"Yes. Many years ago, it was found in the brush along the railroad tracks."

"Who brought it in?" Becca tilted her head slightly, a puzzled look plastered on her face.

"Some guy. I told Kyle it was here. I just assumed he'd told his dad and granddaddy."

"That's strange. Well, I'll take it." Becca pulled out her wallet. "Do you take credit cards?"

"Well, of course I do. What do you think this is? Some backwoods sort of store?" Andy chuckled as he rang up her purchase.

The corners of Becca's mouth pulled up. *This was going be a great day.*

Her next stop was the drugstore. In New York, back in the day, they had Woolworth's. Here in Steam, they had Dickies. She entered the store and looked around. It had all the essentials to get you through until you could make it to the big-box stores about thirty miles away, or if you were so inclined, to Dallas, which was two hours away. She walked up and down the five aisles and then headed to the back where a long lunch counter with chrome and red leather stools lined up. An older, bald fellow stood behind the counter filling up napkin dispensers. He looked up when he heard her footsteps.

She pulled up her hand and waved. "Hi, I'm Becca Parsons."

"I'm Jasper Jennings. We're not open for lunch yet."

"Oh, I'm not here for lunch."

The man's eyes widened. "Oh?"

"I mean, I just had breakfast. I'm visiting Steam and am just checking out the town."

"I see." He continued to fill the dispenser.

"What sort of food do you serve?" Becca walked up closer to the counter.

"Burgers, shakes, that sort of thing." He folded his arms.

Becca raised her hand and waved again. "I'm sorry, I'm keeping you from doing your job. I'll leave you alone. Maybe I'll come back for lunch later."

"You do that. What did you say your name was?"

"Becca. Becca Parsons."

"Oh, you're that city slicker here doing a story on the Huntsman's."

"No, I'm a journalist here providing coverage for the anniversary of the Huntsman story." Becca frowned.

"The Huntsman family are good people. Don't do anything to hurt them."

"I wouldn't dream of hurting them. Who told you that I would?"

"Well … Kyle said—"

Becca put her hand up to stop him. "Listen, Kyle is wrong. He misunderstood. He'll fix this. Thanks for your time." She rushed out of the drugstore and headed back to get her rental car. It was time for a visit with Kyle—cracked ribs, gashed forehead, and all.

CHAPTER 9

Kyle moved slowly into the kitchen to pour a cup of coffee. Determined, or more likely too stubborn to let anyone get it for him, he moaned and groaned as he got the cup down from the cabinet.

Granddaddy sat at the table peering over the top of the daily paper, as his grandson's stubbornness almost got the best of him. "Need any help?"

"No, I got it," Kyle grunted.

Granddaddy shook his head and continued to read the paper.

Kyle shuffled over to the table carrying his mug and pulled a chair back, sliding in slowly. "Ouch."

Granddaddy folded the paper and set it aside. "Man, you're stubborn as a goat."

Kyle laughed. "Granddaddy, I can't lie in bed any

longer. I have to see something besides the four walls of my bedroom." He pulled the cup to his lips and blew before tasting. "Ooh, this coffee tastes good." He leaned back.

"It's just a couple of days. The doc said to give it—"

Kyle interrupted him. "I know what he said."

Granddaddy pushed his chair back and stood. "Well, I'm going out for a walk before the day sets in. I suppose you'll be alright?" He raised his brows.

"Yes. Yes, I'll be alright. I wish everyone would stop babying me."

Granddaddy worked his way over to Kyle and stood behind him. Laying both hands on his shoulders, he gently squeezed. "Boy, we are a little sensitive around here with all the losses we've endured. It's not babying as much as it is protecting the ones we love."

Kyle started to turn in his chair but was suddenly reminded of his limitations and grimaced. "Thanks. I love you, too."

Granddaddy grabbed his old straw hat off of the coat-tree, and when Kyle heard the screen door slam and bounce a few times, he listened to make sure Granddaddy made it off the porch safely. He counted each step in his head—one, two, three. Picking up his coffee mug, he took a sip, then another before leaning back and closing his eyes. As much as he hated to admit it, he'd have to take some pain medication to get through the day.

He finished his coffee and then fixed a bowl of cereal

for breakfast. When he finished eating, he waddled back down the hall to his room to get dressed. He eyed the blue jeans hanging over the back of a chair in the corner. *This is going to be fun.* Deciding against the jeans, he opened a dresser drawer and pulled out a pair of black gym shorts with a wide elastic band and the largest T-shirt he owned. By sitting on the edge of the bed, he managed to pull on the shorts first, and then very carefully slipped the T-shirt over his head. Breathing heavily just from dressing, Kyle made his way down the hallway and to the living room where he planned to sit on the couch most of the day, watching television. A knock on the door changed his course, and he answered it instead.

"Becca!" His eyes widened.

She blew past him, and with folded arms, shot darts at him from her angry eyes.

"What's wrong?" He moved closer.

"I just met two people in town who think I'm a low-life reporter here to disparage your family!" A tear dropped onto her bottom lid and wiggled there a moment before trailing down her cheek. She quickly wiped it away. "How could you tell people that about me?" Her bottom lip trembled.

He moved even closer now, wrapping his arms around her. "Baby, don't be mad. That was then. I'll fix it. I promise." He pulled her in and kissed the top of her head.

"Kyle Huntsman, don't." She pulled out of his reach.

He brushed his hand through his hair and then shook his head. "Damn it, Becca. What do you want from me? I told you I'd fix it. Give me a chance to do that. I'm currently out of commission." He balled up his fist and hit the side of the couch.

Her eyes widened with surprise. "Okay, I'm sorry. It's just that I came back to Steam and thought, hey, I'll look around, make some friends. You know, in case …"

"In case what?" His eyes bored holes right to her soul.

"I don't know." She hung her head low.

He raised her chin with his fingers. "Becca?"

"I don't know." She heaved her shoulders. "I was thinking maybe I'd stay awhile." She raised her eyes to meet his.

He gulped. "Do you mean it? You'd give up New York for Steam?" His eyes darted from her forehead to her mouth and back to her eyes.

She nodded. "The thought had crossed my mind." She looked down at her new cowboy boots and wiggled her toes.

He slipped his hands around her waist and tugged her in for a hug. "I'd love it if you stayed for a while," he whispered in her ear.

She shivered at his sweet warm voice.

"Granddaddy went for a walk," he nibbled on her ear, causing her to almost melt into his arms.

She pulled back slightly so they'd be face-to-face. Taking a breath, her lips met his with an urgency they both felt. As his tongue swept the inside of her mouth she responded by pulling him tighter against her body. He groaned then he cried out in pain.

"What?" She pulled back quickly.

"My ribs. Damn, I think I need a pain pill."

"Where are they?"

He directed her to the cabinet in the kitchen, but she found the bottle sitting on the counter.

"Are you sure you didn't take your dose already this morning?" She held the bottle in her hand as she read the label. It said every six to eight hours.

He vehemently shook his head. "I got sidetracked. I didn't take it."

She popped the lid, shook a pill into his hand, and then filled a glass with water for him.

"Where can I write down that you took this pill?" She searched for a log of some sort.

"I don't. I just remember when I took it."

"Kyle, no, you don't remember. You just said you got sidetracked. This is a serious, heavy-duty narcotic. You must remember to log this somewhere." She crossed her arms across her chest and tapped her toe. "I've covered narcotic stories before. I know what I'm talking about."

He shuffled over to the catchall drawer in the kitchen and pulled out a tablet and pen, shoving them toward her. "Write it down here." He crossed the room to the living room and slowly eased down into the cushions.

Becca joined him and reached over to take his hand in

hers. "I don't want anything to happen to you. Those are heavy-duty pills. I want you to get better so we can start where we left off." She laced her arm through his and laid her head on his shoulder.

"I know. I was being a bit careless. I'm not really that way. I guess the pain has fried some of my brain cells."

"Well, I'd rather the pain be the culprit than the pills. They can do all sorts of damage, too." She blinked, fluttering her long lashes at him.

"I really don't like how they make me feel. But it does take the edge off of the pain." He opened up to her.

"I know. I hate even taking aspirin. I've found that essential oils do a lot of what pharmaceuticals can do. Are you willing to give them a try?" She batted her lashes again.

"Essential oils? What are those?"

"You know, like lavender, peppermint, frankincense."

He laughed out loud. "No, I don't. But I guess you're going to try them on me anyway."

"I brought my emergency kit with me. I don't leave home without them. I'll bring some over tonight."

"Tonight?" He arched his brows to his hairline.

"If you want to see me, that is. I have to leave tomorrow and go back to New York."

He looked down at his lap for a moment then slowly raised his head and turned to look at her. "I want to see you as much as I can. I'm sorry about the accident and messing up your trip out here."

She patted his arm. "Oh, Kyle, it's not your fault. That darn deer ran out in front of you. You couldn't help it. I'm just glad you're okay." She lifted up slightly and kissed his forehead.

A warm smile crossed her face and she stood up brushing her hands down her legs. "You didn't even notice my new boots."

"Yes, I did. They're super sexy, just like you." He reached for her hands.

She helped him stand, and then slipped her arms around him. "I'll be back later. Try to get some rest."

He walked her to the front door, where they heard someone coming up on the porch. "Granddaddy coming back from his walk."

"Oh, hey, Becca. Nice to see you." Granddaddy rubbed his hand up and down her arm and then tossed his hat on one of the hooks.

"Hello, Dirk. Did you have a nice walk?"

He nodded. "I did. It started out cool, but the sun is making an appearance and warming things up." He unbuttoned his old, tattered, red and black thermal jacket and tossed it on an empty hook.

"I'll come back tonight for another visit. We can talk then." She exited the house and stood on the porch.

Kyle held onto the door frame and smiled at her, tilting his head slightly. "See you tonight."

CHAPTER 10

She sat in her car, frozen for a moment as she stared at him leaning against the wooden door frame, looking too damn sexy for his own good. She passed her tongue over her lips as she drew in a deep breath. Resisting him would be harder than she'd ever guessed. She gave him a last-minute wave and then took off out of the driveway, dust billowing all around her.

In a complete daze, Becca drove back to the hotel, where she turned on the television, mainly for some background noise as she began to pack. As much as she dreaded leaving Steam, her life was back in New York City.

She closed her suitcase and set it near the door. She bounced a couple of times on the springy bed while chewing the inside of her mouth. If she was in New York, there would be plenty to do. She reached for her phone and called Jessica.

"Hey, Becca. How are things going in Steam?"

"Fine, I guess," she quipped.

"Are you heading back tomorrow?" Jessica tried to pull more words from her.

"Yeah," she said, sighing into the receiver.

"Okay, what's wrong?" Jessica blurted.

"I guess I'd hoped something would have happened between Kyle and me to let me know if these feelings are real or unfounded."

"He got into an accident, Becca. That changed a few things."

Becca could hear the frustration in her friend's voice. "I know. But I still hoped he would have said or done more to let me know where I stand."

"He told you he missed you. You said the kisses were heartfelt. Not sure what else you were expecting."

"I guess. Well, I'm off to find a burger. Have a good rest of your day. See you when you get back from Alaska."

SHE PARKED along the tree-lined sidewalk and hit the key fob to lock her doors. She turned when she realized how silly that was. This was Steam, Texas, with a population of three thousand,. She hit the fob once more to unlock the doors and made her way to the drugstore. She slid onto a red swivel stool and picked up one of the plastic coated bifold menus.

"I'll be with you in a second," Jasper called out with his back turned to Becca.

"Take your time," she answered. "I'm still debating between the cheeseburger and the BLT." She giggled.

Jasper spun around. "Oh, it's you."

Becca peered over the menu and arched her brows. "Yup."

He crossed over to the counter and gave the top a quick wipe with his cleaning cloth. "Both choices are good."

Becca laid the menu down. "I think I'll have the cheeseburger with extra pickles and a chocolate shake."

He wrote down her order and then clipped it to the line and spun it to the back where the kitchen was located. She could hear some water running from the back and the sizzling of her burger as it was being cooked.

"So, who's your short-order cook?" Becca smiled.

"Oh, that's my wife, Lula May. We've run this little place since nineteen eighty-six. Before that, it was owned by her parents."

"Oh, that's nice. Who will get to run it after you both are gone?" She raised the water glass to her lips and tasted the refreshing drink.

"Unfortunately, no one. We'll sell. In fact, we're

talking retirement." He quickly turned away from her and began to straighten up the other side of the counter.

"I'm leaving tomorrow. Is there anything more you can add to the disappearance of Dirk's folks?" Becca asked.

Jasper shook his head.

"Do you really think they just vanished into thin air?"

Jasper shrugged.

"Aren't you curious about the story at all?" Becca prodded.

Jasper turned around and leaned against the counter across from her. His deep stare made the hair on the back of her neck stand straight up.

She shuddered. "I mean, it seems that someone should know something, or at least have a theory."

"Right." He suddenly turned when he heard his wife say the burger was up. He slid the plate to her. "Ketchup? Mustard?"

"Mayo," she answered.

He moved over to the stainless steel fridge and opened it, retrieving the gallon sized jar. He scooped a small amount into a condiment paper cup.

"Thanks," she replied in a low voice.

"Can I get you anything else?" He raised his brows.

"No, this is good." She picked up the burger and took a bite. She chewed for a moment and then covered her mouth, and with muffled sounds said, "This burger is delicious."

"Thanks. I'll give your compliments to the chef." His eyes twinkled which made Becca feel more comfortable.

"By the way," Becca said in between bites. "Do you know anyone here in town that is still alive that knew Dirk's family personally?"

Jasper's shoulders slumped. "Spencer."

Becca's eyes widened. "Oh?"

Jasper crossed over to the counter and folded his arms across his chest. "He lives at the very edge of town. Almost out of town, really."

"Why didn't you mention that before?" She cocked her head as she waited.

"Because you didn't ask me." He busily began to wipe all the stainless-steel surfaces down with some blue solution in a spray bottle and a towel.

Becca finished her burger and shake. Her next stop— Andy Taylor at the antique shop.

The hanging chimes clattered as she entered the dark and dusty store. A surprise sneeze escaped her, causing her to frantically search for a tissue in her deep hole of a purse.

"Bless you."

"Thank you," she said, blotting her nose.

"What brings you back so soon? I don't give any refunds," he sang out.

"Oh, I'm not here to get my money back for the Bible. I just popped in to say hello."

Andy quirked a smile.

She pretended to be looking at items on a shelf. He stood nearby watching her every move.

She held up a figurine with chipped paint. "This is interesting." She set it back on the shelf. "Do you know Spencer?"

"Of course. Everyone in Steam knows of him. He's a loner. He's never been married, used to live with his momma, and folks say he's got a screw loose. You know, not playing with a full deck." He arched his brows.

"Oh, I see."

"He's older than dirt too and on his last leg here in this world."

"Jasper over at Dickies said he may be the last remaining person in Steam to know Dirk's family."

"Yep, and he's about to kick the bucket. What's your point?"

"I just thought maybe he could add something about the disappearance." She studied another object on the shelf, trying to make out what it was.

"Don't you think the cops have interviewed everyone here more than once?" Andy knitted his brows then brushed his hand over his chin.

She nodded. "Well, sometimes people decide to open up more, especially when they know they're about to pass away. It's like cleaning your soul." She pursed her lips tightly.

"Maybe, but I doubt it." He turned away and walked back to the counter.

"Well, have a nice day, Andy."

Becca got into her car and sat for a moment as she contemplated her next move. The investigative reporter in her told her exactly what her next step should be.

The house was in complete shambles. Roof tiles were missing, the porch was all but collapsed, and the vegetation was so overgrown, it looked like no one lived in the house. Well, no one but an eighty-eight-year-old dying man.

She carefully maneuvered the dry rotten stairs and gingerly walked across the dilapidated porch to the front door. Not really expecting anyone to answer, she still rapped on the door a couple of times. When no one came, she tried the doorknob, and it turned in her hand. Slowly, she pushed the well-worn-door open, which creaked alerting anyone inside that she was coming in.

"Hello? Hello?"

No reply.

She quickly looked around the room—a sofa, one chair, a couple of mismatched tables, and a frayed, braided rug. In the back there was a chrome dinette set reminiscent of the forties. "Hello, anyone home?"

She heard some rustling coming from the back of the house. "Hello, I'm Becca Parsons. Spencer?"

Coughing from a back bedroom directed her down a short hall. Inside the first door, she found a frail man in a dark blue robe and brown slippers sitting in a gold colored upholstered chair.

"Spencer?"

"Yes," he choked out.

"My name is Becca Parsons. I'm a friend of Kyle Huntsman."

He lowered his gaze.

She took a few steps inside the room. "I was visiting Steam during the festival when I met Kyle."

He coughed into a dark colored handkerchief.

"I don't mean to bombard you with questions, but I heard you may have known Dirk and his family."

He shook his head. "No, I didn't."

Becca scrunched up her face. "You weren't friends with the Huntsman family, ever?"

He lifted his shaky head and tried to make eye contact with Becca.

"You're not in any trouble, Spencer. I'm a friend of Kyle's."

"They roughed me up a bit, took my Bible, and threw it into the trees. Gave me a black eye and took my nickel that I had in my pocket."

Becca gasped. "Who did?"

"Three guys on the tracks," he whispered.

"Three guys? The Bible you mentioned, where did you get that from?"

"Dirk's momma gave it to me. Said she wanted me to read it."

"So, you did know the Huntsman family. Do you

remember anything unusual happening the day they disappeared?"

"Just that I saw Dirk that day playing on the tracks. I was sitting in the bushes reading my bible when I saw him."

"When did you come across the teens who beat you up?" Becca asked him slowly and without raising her voice.

"Later. I was on my way home when they came up on me."

"You'd never seen them before?" She kept the questions coming.

He shook his head. "They were mean boys."

Becca thought fast. It could just be a mere coincidence about these boys just like everyone in Steam said.

"Well, I guess it will remain a mystery for all time about Dirk's momma and daddy." She started to step away from him.

"Dirk's daddy had a gambling problem. People say someone came to collect the debt."

Becca stood motionless.

"His momma was a God-fearing woman, though."

Becca relaxed her stance. "I bet she was. I guess she was very fond of you."

He produced a weary smile. "I really liked the Huntsman family."

"Take care, Spencer." She lightly brushed her hand down his arm.

The old man nodded off and began to snore. Becca quietly left the room and house and soon was on the road to Kyle's.

He gave her a quick peck on the cheek then headed back to the couch.

"Why didn't you tell me about Spencer?"

He leaned back into the corner of the couch and peered at her through squinted lids. "Why would I?"

"Why? Because he knew your great-grandparents. He met the same thugs on the tracks that day, but he insists there were three, not two. He said he saw your granddaddy."

"I think he's confused about how many. I didn't tell you because there is no proof that he knows anything, and all you'd be doing is perpetuating rumors. I thought we already had this discussion."

Her hands flew up, and her temper flared before she could control it. "I care about you and your family. I'm just trying to get answers, is all. You may think he doesn't know what he's talking about, but if there were three guys that could be the missing link." She headed to the front door.

"See this is why it'll never work between us. You city folks go off half-cocked and we just—"

"Want to keep your head in the sand?" She finished his sentence.

"Now, wait a minute." He stood and crossed over to her.

She crossed her arms.

He reached out and touched her. "Let's start over."

A tear rolled down her cheek without any warning. She quickly brushed it away. "It's a little late for that, isn't it?"

He led her back to the couch. "Sit."

With her arms still crossed, and now pouting, she sat.

He sat next to her. "I didn't share with you about Spencer because, truthfully, it's an ongoing investigation and really shouldn't be talked about, especially with non-family members. I don't think you should interfere as this is a family matter, although I do appreciate your concern." He gazed at her with affection. "I'm sorry if I upset you. That wasn't my intention," he said, lowering his voice by several octaves and softening his stare. "What all did he tell you?"

She turned to study his face, and ran her tongue along her bottom lip. Even when she was most angry at him, she still wanted him. "He just said he ran across some thugs on the tracks, and they beat him up and took his Bible."

Kyle nodded. "The Bible you purchased from Andy?"

Her eyes widened. "How'd you know that?"

"Remember, this is a small town."

"And a gossipy one, at that." She smirked.

"Andy just wanted me to know. I knew that it was a gift from my great-grandparents. And I also knew it was found near the tracks. But, it belongs to Spencer, though."

"So, you think Spencer ran across that same bunch, or different ones?"

"Probably the same ones. The difference was, Granddaddy could run fast, and Spencer, being a little on the slow side, didn't see the danger."

"Okay." She snuggled closer to him. "Now that we've made up, can I have a kiss?"

He tossed his arm over her shoulders and pulled her close. "Just be careful of the merchandise. I'm trying to get better so we can do more than just kiss." He winked then covered her mouth with his.

After the kiss, Becca's head whirled even more. Should she go? Should she stay? Her job, apartment, and whole life were in New York. She sighed. Why did this have to happen?

"I'm going to go back to the hotel and edit my story to include my discussion with Spencer."

He nibbled on her earlobe, kicking up her pulse a notch, which pounded in her ears. "Sure," he mumbled. Then he suddenly pulled away. "Let me read it first, though." He narrowed his eyes.

She cupped his face with her hands, fervently searching his face. "Kyle, what about us?"

He pulled up and raised his brows. "What about us?" He flashed a warm smile, showing off his dimple.

She wanted to kiss it, run her tongue along it; it was that juicy. She gulped. "Us. You know, do we have a future?"

He sighed. "I don't know. Do you plan to move to Steam?" His eyes twinkled.

"I thought about it. Would you like me to?"

"You aren't really serious about moving here, are you? We don't have fancy stores, no fine dining, and our theater plays shows that have already run the circuit." His voice stayed even with no signs of emotion, almost making her wish she hadn't said it.

"I know I'd be giving up a lot. Not to mention my career. But I feel something for you I haven't felt in a long time." She picked up his hands and circled his thumbs with hers.

"Yeah, I'd never give up my life here in Steam. So, I'm not sure I could ask you to do the same."

He was showing more signs of being noncommittal, making her suddenly nervous. She let go of his hands. "Really? You wouldn't give up something for another person? Now who's being like a city slicker?" She stood.

"Oh, geeze, not again." He stood and grabbed her around the waist, twirling her around.

"Don't touch me. I may not be worth the effort." Another tear trickled down her cheek.

"Becca, it came out wrong. I just don't want you

doing something you'll regret. Just sleep on it. I don't want to be the reason there isn't an us."

She relaxed her shoulders, and moving her head to and fro, shook off the tension. "Okay. I'm going back to the hotel. This day has been something else." She leaned in and kissed him on the mouth.

"Are you still heading back to New York tomorrow?" He walked her to the door.

"Jack had said I could stay for a few days to get more of the story, but there doesn't seem to be any more story. I'll just add the little bit about Spencer, if that's okay?"

"Jack?" he asked with a puzzled look.

"He's my boss."

"Oh. So, you are heading back?"

"Yes, sadly tomorrow." She tightly pressed together her lips. "I hope you'll come visit me in New York?"

He nodded. "I will. Let me just get over this injury. I'll be in touch."

"Bye, Kyle. Tell your dad and granddaddy goodbye for me. Maybe you can bring them to New York, too? I'd love to show them around. I might have someone your dad would be interested in." Her mind went to the oldest employee in the office, a veteran journalist who'd been around the block a few times.

Kyle chuckled. "Maybe."

Becca turned and began to exit the house, but her movement came to a complete halt when Kyle's strong hands whirled her around and into his arms. Finding his warm mouth ready and waiting for her, she feverishly kissed him as she wrapped her arms around his neck, holding him tightly in place. He groaned as she ran her fingers through his hair. Reluctantly, they pulled apart, breathing heavily.

"I'm going to miss you," he said, his eyes deep and inviting and his dimple proudly revealed.

"I'll miss you, too."

Before she headed back to the hotel, she drove quickly back to Spencer's. He was still resting when she entered the house. Not wanting to wake him, she put the tiny Bible on his lap and then placed his hand on top to keep it from slipping. As she stepped back to exit the room, he began making mumbling noises. Slowly, his eyes opened.

"Hey, Spencer. It's Becca again, Kyle's friend. I wanted to give you something before I left Steam." She tipped her head toward his lap.

He fingered the leather-bound Bible, and then with shaky hands, drew it up close to his face so he could see it. A slow smile crossed his face and he hugged it to his chest, as a tear rolled down his cheek. "Thank you."

"You're welcome. Take care," she said softly.

CHAPTER 11

Becca gazed out the airplane window as it backed away from the gate. Leaning back in her comfy first-class seat, she waited for the plane to take off before she settled in to read and listen to music. The image of Spencer when he recognized his Bible was forever etched in her mind. She sighed recalling the image. A few rows ahead, she heard the flight attendant taking drink orders, and she waited patiently for her turn.

"I'll have a Bloody Mary," she told the cheerful attendant.

Soon the plane was soaring at its cruising altitude, and she leaned back, inserted her earplugs, and listened to relaxing music that hopefully would take away her pain. But every time she closed her eyes, she saw Kyle.

After a couple of hours, the plane landed at JFK Airport. She retrieved her suitcase and hailed a taxi. The taxi ride to her apartment was surreal. The land of quiet had calmed her nerves, and she didn't realize until now just how much all the hustle and bustle of the big city could wear on one's soul. She sighed. The taxi driver pulled up in front of her high-rise apartment building, and helped her with her luggage. She tipped him, and headed for the rotating glass doors, where the doorman stood nearby.

"Hello, Rich."

"Good day, Ms. Parsons." He tipped his head and smiled.

She entered the lobby and made her way toward the row of brass colored mailboxes to retrieve her mail. Securing it under her arm, she headed to the elevator and punched the button for the fifteenth floor. Rolling her suitcase along behind her, she ambled down the long hallway until she reached her door. Inside, she tossed the mail onto a table and made her way toward the back of the apartment to its only bedroom. Sitting on the edge of the bed, she stared into space for a moment, then cupped her face and began to bawl. Once her tears subsided, she felt she'd had a much needed stress relieving cry. Now all she needed was a shower.

JESSICA WRAPPED her arms around Becca and gave her a hug. "I missed you, girl!"

Becca tossed her purse into her desk drawer and sat in her rolling desk chair. "Thanks. I missed you, too." She turned on her computer.

"Well?"

Becca looked up at Jessica who remained standing after the hug. "Well, what?"

"Kyle. That's what." She widened her smile.

"Oh, yeah. Kyle." She hit a few keys on her keyboard and leaned in closer toward the monitor, reading her mail.

"Becca, did something happen between you two?" Jessica crossed her arms.

She laughed out loud. "I guess you could say that. But it doesn't really matter. He's there, and I'm here."

Jessica pulled up her chair and sat. "I know all of that. But I thought …" She tapped her leg.

"It was great, we fit like a glove, and we have chemistry and all of that. But the logistics just don't make us a couple. I'm not into long-distance relationships, and I doubt he is either. I tossed the idea around about me moving there, but he didn't seem all that interested. But I did invite him to visit. I guess the ball's in his court." She shrugged.

Jessica rolled her chair with her feet back to her desk and pulled it closer to her work station. "I guess so. I'm sorry it didn't work out. I was kind of hoping it would."

Becca glanced over at her. "Why?"

She raised her shoulders. "Something about him

being a deputy in a small Texas town and you being this sexy New York journalist just screams romance, and I was really rooting for you guys."

"You read too many romance novels, Jessica!"

"You have to admit the guys here are just not exciting anymore. They're briefcase carrying, suit wearing stuffed shirts." Jessica lifted one shoulder and raised her brows.

"True. That or they're just after one thing. I'm tired of the meat market atmosphere."

"Good morning, Becca," Jack said, startling them both.

"Good morning, Jack." Becca quickly slid back her chair and stood.

"Sit down. This isn't the military." He laughed.

Becca sat.

"How was your trip? Did you get everything you needed?" He winked.

Becca felt her face heat up. "Ahh, yes, I did. I'll have the story on your desk by noon."

"No worries and no hurry. Glad to see you back." He rested his hand on her shoulder.

She looked up at him as he moved away, greeting the next employee down the line.

"I think he's handsome," Jessica whispered.

"Dating the boss is never a good idea, Jessica."

"I'm not saying I would, but an office romance is kind of sexy." She smiled.

"Like I said, too many romance novels." Becca knitted her brows and went back to reading her email.

SHE LIGHTLY RAPPED on Jack's office door and waited.

"Come in," he bellowed.

"Jack, you wanted to see me?"

"Yes, have a seat," he said, motioning to the black leather chairs front and center of his large desk.

She smoothed out her black skirt, crossed her feet at the ankles, and clasped her hands in her lap as she looked up and smiled at Jack.

"I like the story. You did a great job considering there really hasn't been any progress made in years." He leaned back in his chair.

"Thanks. It was pretty much a dead-end story. I thought I found another lead but turns out it was already in the files." She rocked her head back and forth while shrugging.

"So for your next assignment, I wondered if you'd like to go to Hawaii."

"Hawaii, sir? Sure. What's the scoop?"

"A little R & R."

She knitted her brows and cocked her head. "R & R? I don't understand."

"I have a villa there overlooking the ocean. You'd be my guest."

Becca's hand flew to her mouth. She quickly recovered. "Oh, that's very kind of you, but no thank you. I just got back and …"

He pushed his chair back and came around in front, leaning up against the desk. "I know you just came back. I'm gathering that since you are back, things didn't work out with the sheriff?"

Becca scowled. "Since when do chief editors and bosses care if things worked out with other people or not?" She crossed her arms across her chest in a protective mode and in protest of his inappropriate line of questioning.

He tossed his head back and deeply laughed. "I just thought we had a connection. I guess I read you wrong." He winked.

All kinds of crazy thoughts raced through her head. She wanted to tell him to jump off the cliff that overlooked his villa. She wanted to add that she felt he was being totally tasteless in how he was speaking and acting with her. Talk about putting on the pressure. And what about Jessica? She really wanted to romp in the hay with him, and yet he had picked her for the romp. She sighed.

"Really? You thought we had some sort of connection? I've never heard anything more ridiculous in my life. I don't even really know you. One minute I'm on assignment and the next thing I know, I have a new boss. One that lacks work ethics, I might add. No, please don't flatter yourself. I'm not interested in dating my boss. She stood. "Thanks for the offer, but I'll have to decline." With her back turned, she took a few steps toward the door. She stopped and looked over her shoulder. "Oh, and take this as my resignation. I'll have it to you in writing by of the end of the day."

"Becca, wait. You'd quit your job just because of a little misunderstanding?"

"Oh, please. Don't put yourself up on such a high pedestal. I'm resigning because I'm moving to Steam, Texas. You just helped me make the decision easier. I've been trying to find a way to get out of this rut.

"Rut?" I thought you liked your job here?"

"I do. I did. But I also discovered that I'm really tired of the city life, working for men—and dating some, who think they are the cat's meow. This just helped me finalize my thoughts and help me move forward. I really should be thanking you."

With one hand on the door she hesitated before opening it. She slowly turned to face him. "Oh and by the way, I'll be looking for a generous departing package."

"Wait, you don't get…"

She wrinkled her brows stopping him.

"Oh you're a clever one. So you want me to say that you're being laid off?"

"Wow, you're actually smarter than you look." She pulled the door open and stepped out closing it behind her. A snarky little smile pulled up at the corners of her lips. She hated he pushed her to the limits, but there's only so much a girl can take. She held her head high and walked toward her desk.

BECCA SLAMMED HER DESK DRAWER, tossed her pencils and pens around, and plucked at her keyboard so loudly she was drawing some attention.

"What did he want?" Jessica smiled as she waited.

"He's a jerk. He came on to me."

Jessica's eyes widened like saucers. "What?"

"Yeah, and just so you know, office romances are not always sexy." She plucked at more keys.

"So, what are you going to do?"

"I'm resigning."

"You're kidding, right?"

"Nope. I'm leaving for Steam as soon as I can find someone to sublet my apartment and get packed."

"Take me with you," Jessica yelled.

Becca tilted her head and stared at the creamy porcelain face with bright red lips and twinkling blue eyes. "What?"

"I need an adventure. New York is boring."

"Okay, New York is boring, but you categorize Steam as an adventure? If you don't think there are any eligible bachelors here, what do you think Steam will have?"

"Oh, I don't know. Maybe Kyle has a cousin or something?"

CHAPTER 12

Over drinks, Jessica and Becca discussed their plans. They both agreed they'd had it with New York City. A change was definitely in order for the both of them. But could they handle living in a place with no shopping malls or fine dining? She looked around the dimly lit restaurant with the white linen cloths and in the distance, the beautifully designed mahogany bar. She wrinkled her brow. Nothing like this in Steam, that's for sure.

"Do you think I'm making a mistake?" She twirled the plastic swizzle stick in her martini then popped an olive into her mouth.

"I don't know. I don't think so. It is kind of impulsive, though." Jessica lifted a shoulder and flashed a wide smile.

"I know, and I'm not the impulsive type." She drew the Y-shaped glass to her lips and tasted the drink.

"Well, I don't know about that. You went on a second trip to Steam, and that was kind of impulsive."

Becca looked up at her. "Yeah, I guess."

"Look at it this way. If it doesn't work out, you can always come back to New York." Jessica flashed her wide smile again. "Besides, I'm looking forward to the change of scenery."

"TRUE."

Becca raised her hand to get the server's attention. "Another drink?" she asked Jessica.

"Okay, but then we better order dinner."

"It's a good thing I've been saving for a rainy day," Becca joked as she picked at her dinner.

"It didn't hurt that you came into a little windfall, too." Jessica said, reminding her of the judgement she'd won in a lawsuit.

Becca winked. "Yep, that definitely helped to pave the way for a very nice future for me. But, I had to get down and dirty to make my point."

"Sometimes we have to do that. But it all worked out, and now you're set for life practically. Doesn't it feel good to be able to tell Jack Porter to stick it where the sun doesn't shine, and know that you'll be alright?" She laughed.

Becca joined Jessica in a hearty laugh. "I wouldn't say I'm set for life exactly, but it's a nice little nest egg, and now I know what I was meant to do with it."

Jessica picked up her glass. "Here's to Steam, Texas, winning lawsuits, and finding sexy men in places we never dreamed of."

Becca picked up her glass when Jessica first began her spiel, but then quickly put it down. "Wait … sexy men? You haven't found any sexy man in Steam." She cocked her head and frowned.

"Not yet, honey, but I'm remaining very optimistic." She held out her glass for the toast.

Becca clanked her glass with Jessica's, shaking her head. "You are incorrigible, Jessica." She put the glass to her mouth, tasting the cool drink on her lips, all the while smiling.

"Hey, how are you?"

"Good. It's nice to hear your voice," Kyle said.

"So, are your ribs healed?" She tried to find something to say that didn't involve moving to Steam. Not right away, anyway.

"Yup, I'm as good as new. Doc said I'm a young stud so my recovery time would be fast." He laughed. Becca smiled and her heart began to pump fast and heavy when her naughty mind envisioned his tight abs and broad shoulders, which she couldn't stop thinking about.

"I quit my job," she blurted.

"You did what?"

"Quit my job," she repeated.

"I heard that. But why?"

"Jack came on to me, and I felt it best not to stick around there anymore."

"Well, that son of a … I'll come up there and kick his ass."

The air whooshed from her lungs. She liked this side of him. She already knew he was sexy as all get out, but now his chivalry came through, and over the phone! "Now, Kyle, I took care of it," she said steadying her voice.

"How'd you take care of it? By quitting? That's giving that low-life boss who preys on women the upper hand."

Becca covered the phone so he couldn't hear her excitement. "Well, truthfully, I'd sort of made up my mind to quit, anyway. That was just the icing on the cake."

"So, what are you going to do in the meantime?"

"I thought about moving. A change of scenery might do me good." She paused a second. "I was thinking about moving to Steam." There, she said it.

"Here?"

"Uh-huh," she said in her best sexy tone.

"Well, you know I'd love for you to be closer. I do miss

your quirky big-city attitude. Maybe Dallas would be a better choice? They have super malls and fine dining and—"

She cut him off. "And first run movies. I know all of that. But there's one thing it doesn't have."

"Oh, what's that? Cuz I can't imagine Dallas not having most everything New York has, except maybe friendlier people." He laughed.

"You, silly."

"I can visit you, though."

Disappointed that he wasn't getting the full picture of why she wanted to move to Steam, she threw herself across her bed. "Visiting is not good enough."

"You mean you'd turn me away if I drove all the way to Dallas to see you?" His sexiness came right through the phone and had her heart pounding again.

"I might meet another handsome man there. Then what would you do?" she teased back.

"I don't know. I guess I'd kick his ass and then take you away and make mad, passionate love to you."

A shiver ran up her spine. "Ooh, I like the sounds of that."

"Since you're unemployed, why don't you come out to Steam and visit for a while? See if this is really where you want to hang your hat and kick your boots off."

Now he was getting it. She sat up and slid to the edge of the bed so her feet touched the floor. "Can I bring a friend?"

CHAPTER 13

Jack Porter got the surprise of his life when Jessica walked into his office and told him she was quitting as well.

"I bet his jaw dropped to the floor when you uttered the words severance package" Jessica turned to Becca, who had her feet up on the dashboard, wiggling her freshly painted toes.

Becca laughed out loud. "He had to pick it up right off the ground. But I'm not going to fool around and contact a lawyer. I just wanted him to think that I would. Even though it was for something completely different, one lawsuit in a lifetime is enough."

"I can't believe we're really driving across the United States," Jessica said.

"I think it's great. Two friends driving across the country, talk about an adventure."

Jessica drew in a deep breath. "Don't you just love this new car smell?"

"I do. You made a great choice with this vehicle. I'll probably buy a truck when I get to Steam." She flashed a wide smile.

"A truck? You driving a truck … that's something I have to see."

"Let me know when you get tired and I'll drive." Becca leaned her head back on the headrest and closed her eyes, enjoying the warmth of the sun shining through the windows.

"I figure when we stop for lunch would be a good time to switch. Carbs always make me sleepy."

After a couple of hours, they stopped for lunch. Jessica had a burger and fries—which she'd earned, and Becca had a grilled chicken salad and iced tea. No falling asleep at the wheel for her.

While Jessica rested, Becca drove the next four hours. That would be their final stop for the night. They both agreed they wouldn't drive in the dark, and instead would have a good dinner and get a good night's sleep.

Becca's mind wandered a bit during those four hours. As excited as she was about the possibilities of moving to Steam permanently, she wondered if it would come to fruition. Jessica promised to keep it a secret that they'd sublet their apartments and had packed up all their belongings, which were now being held in storage by the moving company until they were given the final okay to transport them. That way, if Dallas became their new home, their stuff wouldn't be in Steam. Or maybe they wouldn't live in Texas, at all. Any place could be their home. They didn't have any ties to New York. Jessica's family all lived in Wisconsin, and Becca's mother lived in New Jersey. Last she heard, her dad was possibly living in California, and her deadbeat brother, Peter, was somewhere in Canada. She twisted her mouth in contemplation and then looked back in the rearview mirror. Not a single car for miles.

She picked up her cell phone—no cell coverage. She tossed it back onto the center console, and hit the cruise control button to bump up the speed.. She was more anxious than ever to get to Steam.

"Wake up, Jessica. We're here."

Jessica stretched then yawned. "Where is here?" She pulled her sunglasses down and looked around.

"Durham, North Carolina." Becca pulled into the restaurant parking lot.

The two women ordered food and then devoured it, bite by bite. The salad Becca had eaten for lunch was long gone.

"I can't wait to have a nice shower and then hit the sack." Jessica took another bite of her hash brown casserole.

"I know. I'm so exhausted." Becca forked a bite of her scrambled eggs. "This place is really good. I'm glad they serve breakfast all day long." Tipping her head, she picked up a piece of crispy bacon. "Super good." She took a bite.

After dinner, the two girls crashed in the hotel. While Jessica showered, Becca called Kyle.

"We made it to Durham, North Carolina, tonight."

"Great. So, what's your next stop?"

"Birmingham, Alabama," Becca said, matter-of-factly.

"You should make it to Dallas the following day then," he said.

"Yes. We could try to come all the way into Steam, but we'll see. It just depends on how tired we are."

"Well, when you do get here, I have something for you."

Becca's stomach pitched and rolled when she thought of Kyle. She could imagine his alluring brown eyes, his glowing smile, and that cute as a button dimple when he spoke.

"I can't wait to see you and wrap my arms around you," she spoke softly as she twirled a tendril of her hair.

"I can't wait to do more than that. I've thought about you a lot."

"You have?" she teased him for more.

"Yup. Pops and Granddaddy are super excited to see you, too."

Her heart dropped. She wasn't ready for the sexy talk to stop. "I'll be happy to see them, too. But let's go back to what we want to do to each other when we see each other." She arched her brows and waited for more sexual tension to pass through the radio frequency of her cell phone.

"The first thing I'm going to do is pull you into my arms."

"Uh-huh, go on."

"Then I'm going to devour you, inch by inch."

She sighed loudly.

"You like that, do you?" he said in a low gravelly voice.

"I do. Every word."

"Well, you better get some rest. You girls have a long trip ahead. I'll be right here waiting."

"Okay, Kyle. Good night."

Just then, Jessica, wrapped in an oversized bath towel, stepped out of the steamy bathroom. "Tell Kyle I said hi." She sat down on the bed and bounced a couple of times.

"Jessica said hi."

"See you girls soon."

Becca tossed her phone on the nightstand. "Did you leave me any hot water?" She scrounged around in her suitcase for her night clothes.

"Yes," she said matter-of-factly. "How was Kyle?"

"He's excited to see me."

"Just you?" Jessica plopped down on the bed and began to rub lotion on her freshly shaven legs.

Becca leaned into the shower and turned it on, stepping out of her clothes. "I'm sure he can hardly contain his excitement over seeing you," she yelled over the sounds of the water running.

"Oh, go ahead. Be mean."

After Becca finished her shower, she stepped out to finish her conversation with Jessica, only Jessica was sound asleep. She crept quietly to the other side of the bed, making sure she didn't wake her up.

AFTER A GOOD NIGHT'S rest and another hearty meal, the two set off for their next adventure. It was fairly uneventful, except for almost running out of gas. After that, they agreed they'd fill up whenever the tank got down to half full.

They pulled into Birmingham exhausted, and it was another repeat of their first night in a hotel together. While Jessica showered, she got an earful of sweet nothings from Kyle.

On their last night of travel, when she saw the sign indicating Dallas was just a mere twenty miles away, Becca made a command decision to drive straight through to Steam. Jessica, sound asleep with her head smashed up against the window, would never know the difference.

Becca shifted her weight in the seat, wishing she'd stopped to get a cup of coffee. In an effort to remain awake, she turned the air conditioning to high, redirected the vents toward her, and increased the volume on. She turned the radio. , The closer they got to Steam, the darker the roads seemed, and Becca began to worry about running into a deer. The headlights lit up the road pretty well, but she couldn't see what was out in the open land. Just then, she swerved and slammed on the brakes, waking Jessica up abruptly.

"What the heck," she yelled, looking wild-eyed at Becca.

"A coyote ran out from the darkness. I almost hit it," Becca yelled.

Jessica straightened her shoulders and peered out the windshield. "Where the heck are we? This doesn't look like Dallas. Where are the skyscrapers and all the cars and the bright lights of the city?"

"We're almost to Steam."

She rubbed her eyes and then knitted her brows. "Thought we were staying the night in Dallas?"

"I changed my mind." She gripped the steering wheel, and her eyes darted across every stretch of the dark two-lane highway and beyond.

"Okay. How much farther?"

"We're almost to the hotel."

"This is some serious wilderness out here. I mean the highway is so dark and scary." Jessica wrapped her arms around herself.

"Only at night. Oh, here we are." She put on her turn signal and exited the rural stretch of highway.

They pulled into Steam's only hotel, and while Becca checked them in, she left Jessica in the car.

Dangling the keys in her hands, Becca knocked on the passenger side window, startling Jessica. She rolled down the window. "You scared the crap out of me."

"Got the room. Let's go." Becca stood back away from the opening car door.

The two trudged off to their room.

"It's too late to call Kyle. It's after midnight. I'll call in the morning."

"I'm exhausted." Jessica fell onto the queen-sized bed.

"I'm the one who drove the last six hours. I have a right to be tired." She shoved her feet off the bed.

"What did you do that for?" Jessica whined.

"I'm taking my shower first." Becca headed to the bathroom and turned on the faucets. When she stepped into the shower, she let the warm water envelop her. She lathered up, washed her hair, and when she was all dry, she slipped her nightgown over her head. When she walked out of the bathroom, Jessica was snoring softly. Deciding not to wake her, Becca climbed in under the covers and fell fast asleep.

CHAPTER 14

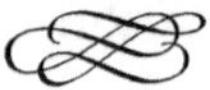

Becca shielded her eyes from the glaring sunlight that danced through the slats of the blinds. She rolled over onto her side, rubbing her eyes. She picked up her cell phone from the bedside table and focused on the time displayed on the screen.

"Wake up, Jessica," she yelled. "It's almost ten o'clock. We've overslept." She pulled the covers off and pushed up against the pillows and headboard. "I never sleep this late."

"Huh?" Jessica rolled over, pulling the covers with her.

Becca gave the covers a yank. "Wake up, sleepy head."

Jessica sighed. "Alright. I was dreaming, and it was a good one."

"Whatever. Get in the shower."

While Jessica took a shower, Becca rummaged through her suitcase to find something to wear, and settled on jeans and a comfy T-shirt with a pair of her new shoes. She decided at the last minute to pull her hair back into a ponytail to show off her dangling turquoise earrings she'd purchased from a gift store at one of their stops along the way to Steam.

"I feel so much better," Jessica said, rubbing her hair dry with a towel.

"Good. I can't wait for you to meet Kyle and his family."

"I need coffee first," Jessica said, frowning.

"Don't worry. I know the perfect diner for that." Becca widened her smile.

The two women made their way to the coffee shop. Becca didn't let Jessica know it was the only one in town. She'd leave that part until later.

"Oh, I remember you," the gum smacking waitress said.

Becca smiled. "Oh, and I remember you," she said snidely, clearly perturbed by her attitude.

"Are you here to see Kyle?"

Becca continued to look at the menu.

"Becca, she was talking to you," Jessica whispered over her menu.

"I'll have a cup of coffee, two pieces of toast, and a side of fruit, please." Becca laid the menu down and tipped her head to Jessica.

"Ahh, let's see. I'll have the same." Jessica handed her menu to the waitress.

"Coming right up," she said curtly as she whooshed away.

"What was that about?"

"Oh, she and Kyle once dated. But I think there may have been more than just dating going on between them. At least, that's what I think. She's too familiar with him."

"Are you jealous?"

"No!"

Just then, the waitress plopped down two white ceramic cups and began to pour coffee from a glass carafe. She pulled out some single-serving creamers and dropped them on the table. "Your food should be out shortly."

"Thank you," Jessica said cheerfully.

Becca frowned at her friend.

"What? I don't feel like eating food that has been spit on by some waitress who you clearly have disdain for, and she you, thank you very much."

Becca crossed her arms. "She wouldn't do that."

"I don't want to take the chance."

"Okay, whatever. So after breakfast," she said, uncrossing her arms and leaning forward, "I'll take you over to the sheriff's office so you can meet Kyle and Robert."

"Robert?"

"His dad," Becca said, crinkling her forehead.

"Oh, that's right, the single dad." She winked at Becca.

"The older, single dad that is too old for you." Becca put her cup of coffee to her lips and drew in a small taste.

"I'll be the judge of that." Jessica also took a sip of her own coffee and then sat back in the booth. "They do make a great cup of coffee here at this diner."

After they ate their breakfast, Becca did just as she told Jessica she would do. They drove over to the sheriff's office.

"Okay, now don't say or do anything stupid," Becca warned her.

"Who me?" Jessica chuckled.

The creaky door announced their visit, and Robert looked up first. He pushed back his chair and crossed over to Kyle's desk and tapped him on the shoulder. Kyle's eyes met hers when he looked up.

She waved. "Hey, guys!"

Kyle and Robert both made their way over to the women.

"This is my best friend, Jessica."

Robert cupped her hand with his. "Nice to meet you, Jessica."

Kyle copied his dad.

After they got the introductions out of the way, Robert rushed over to the other side of the room and produced two chairs on wheels, putting them close to Kyle's desk.

"Have a seat, ladies," he said, motioning toward the chairs.

"How was the trip?" Kyle asked as he leaned against the desk, his legs crossed at the ankles.

Becca couldn't help but notice the long, lean, and muscular shape of his legs and her eyes drew up to his crossed arms that showed more of his muscles. She raised her brows. "The trip was good. We made excellent time."

"Granddaddy is going to be so happy to see you. He's making some of his best dishes for you girls." He winked at her.

Becca crossed her feet at the ankles and stiffened her shoulders trying to stretch out some muscle soreness from the long ride. "That sounds wonderful."

Kyle looked over toward his father and then back to Becca. Holding out his hand, he eased her from her chair and led her to the window in the corner.

"I'm so happy you're here. You're all I've thought about since you left." He squeezed her hand. His eyes, deep and alluring, once again made her palms sweat with desire.

Her words caught and came out hoarse. She swallowed hard and then tried again. "Kyle … I … I don't usually run after guys, especially when they live so far away, but something about you … something about Steam …" She lowered her head.

He lifted her chin with a finger. "I know. It calls for you to come back." His voice, low and sexy, made her heart jump into high gear. "Are you going to stay?" His eyes bore right through her.

"I want to."

"Then do." He pulled her into a hug.

She wrapped her hands behind his back and held him, drawing in the smell of his freshly starched shirt, and his aftershave. Closing her eyes, she pictured them together.

"I guess you need to find a place to live. We don't have any fancy apartment buildings here like in Dallas."

"I was afraid of that. Jessica might stay, too. She's drifting now as well." Becca looked over her shoulder and saw Robert and Jessica talking nonstop.

"You can stay with us until we figure out something."

Becca wasn't sure if she could resist Kyle, living under the same roof. It might be too much for her. "I don't know if that is wise." She smiled up at him.

His low groan let her know he agreed.

"THIS IS SO NICE, sitting out here on the back deck and taking in the lovely views," Becca said.

"And taking in the wonderful smell of grilled beef," Jessica added.

Granddaddy had marinated a tri-tip in his special marinade, and Robert and Kyle were the masters of the grill. Every time, it sizzled and flamed up, Kyle would jump up, armed with his water bottle, and spray down the shooting flames.

"I made coleslaw, hushpuppies, and my famous baked beans," Granddaddy said with a twinkle in his eyes.

"Sounds great," Becca said, smiling at him.

They sat around the wooden picnic table covered in a bright red vinyl tablecloth and shared the delicious meal.

After the scrumptious meal, the girls helped clear the table and put the leftovers away. When the kitchen was cleaned the way Granddaddy liked it, they all went out to the front porch and sat in the big rockers lined up along the house.

"This is the life. A back deck that looks out to the prairie and beyond, and rockers out on the front porch where you can see for miles. I love it." Jessica rocked back and forth.

Becca looked toward Jessica. "I told you it was peaceful."

"I'm stuffed." Jessica rubbed her belly.

"I know. It's hard to push the food away here. I totally will have to exercise a lot to keep the pounds away." Becca rocked in rhythm with Jessica.

Kyle leaned in and whispered something in Becca's ear. She giggled. If only he knew how much she would enjoy his arms wrapped around her. Consider it exercise or recreational enjoyment. Either summed it up quite well.

"So, you like Steam well enough to stick around, Jessica?" Kyle asked.

"Yeah, I think I do. I'm just not sure what Becca and I can do to make a living out here. I don't think you have much demand for journalists." She laughed.

"How about running a lunch counter and drugstore?" Robert asked.

Becca stopped rocking. "You mean Dickies?"

ecca grabbed Jessica by the shoulders and looked her squarely in the eyes. "You know what this means, don't you?"

Jessica arched her brow. "That we are going to be partners?"

Becca grabbed her hands and danced around the room with her. "Yes, and we'll be living here in Steam."

"Okay, hold your horses. Hey, see how I just threw that in and here we are in Texas—"

"Shut it, Jessica. I get it. What's on your mind?" Becca let go of her hands and stepped back with her arms crossed.

"I mean things are going a bit fast. I said I'd come out here since I was unemployed and would check things out. I never made the decision to permanently plant myself here in Dust Bowl, Texas." She turned her back on Becca.

"First of all, that's not very nice to say about Steam. And secondly, you did allude to the idea of maybe trying to live here. That's why I brought you out with me." She walked around Jessica in order to face her again.

"I know," she said.

"Well? What changed your mind? I thought you and Robert hit it off, even though I'm not sure about starting anything with him, just so you know." She gave her a disapproving look.

Jessica swatted her hand. "Oh, that. That's not serious. We just laugh at each other's jokes, enjoy each other's company, and …"

"So, what if you go back to New York and I stay here? I'll plunge right in to being the owner of Dickies, and you can be a silent partner? I can't do it financially all by myself." She tilted her head and gave Jessica a puppy dog look.

"Oh, I hate it when you do that." She smiled.

"I want to stay. I'm crazy about Kyle, and I want to see where it takes us. There's nothing in New York for me anymore."

"Me either, really. I guess I'm just scared about taking such a leap."

"Oh, come on, Jessica. Be my partner. It'll be fun. I have some ideas already to make Dickies the happening place in Steam. In fact, maybe for miles around."

"Well, the first thing in order is a name change. Two attractive single women cannot be the owners and operators of a place called Dickies," Jessica said, crossing her arms.

Becca lifted her brows and then broke into a wide smile then a hearty laugh. Soon Jessica joined her, and they were falling over and grabbing their sides from the pain.

After they regained their composure, another serious topic surfaced. Where would they live while running the new business?

"Okay, so we have a couple of options. There is a small apartment above the drugstore that one of us could live in. The other would have to find another place. It's too small for the both of us," Becca said, now sitting on the edge of the bed.

"If it was big enough for Jasper and Lula May, why wouldn't it be large enough for us?"

"Because just our clothes alone would fill one room."

"True," Jessica said, nodding.

"The store is pretty well in order, we just want to spruce it up some, add to the inventory, maybe fix up the lunch counter a little, add some New York flare to the menu, that sort of thing," Becca said.

"You mean no one here would appreciate sushi?" She laughed.

"Drive to Dallas for all of that," Becca said, standing.

"Okay, so we'll buy the store. Man, I can't believe

we're really doing this," Jessica said, now standing next to Becca.

"It's going to be great. I can't wait to tell Kyle we made a decision. I hope you don't mind hanging out alone tonight. He's picking me up ..." She glanced at her watch. "In exactly one hour! I better get ready." She headed toward the bathroom.

"Hey," Jessica called out.

Becca turned and looked up.

"What makes you think I'm sitting alone in this hotel room?" She lifted her shoulder and tightly pursed her lips, daring Becca to challenge her.

"Robert?"

Jessica nodded. "Yep. He wants to show me around."

"That'll take all of twenty minutes," Becca said, looking back through her suitcase.

"He said the next town over had a great Italian restaurant. We're going there for dinner and drinks."

"Okay, Jessica. I'd tell you not to do anything I wouldn't do, but that just doesn't seem appropriate anymore. I just moved clear across the United States to a small Texas town and am about to buy a drugstore and give my heart to a cowboy deputy sheriff." She shrugged.

Jessica covered her mouth to conceal her joy.

BECCA DRESSED CASUALLY for their date night. She

couldn't imagine that anywhere he'd take her would require more than jeans, a cute top, and of course her new favorite boots. She had to admit, she really loved them!

When Kyle arrived, Jessica was in the bathroom primping, so Becca shouted a goodbye and walked arm in arm to the truck with the cutest lawman in all of Texas. Well, at least she thought so.

"Where are we going?" She asked as she buckled her seatbelt.

"It's a surprise. I know you city girls love the nightlife, and Steam just doesn't have it."

Becca's eyes grew to the size of saucers. "You're taking me to Dallas?"

"No, not Dallas, but hopefully it will suffice until I take you there someday." He winked and then placed his hand on her knee, sending waves of heat running through her entire body.

He raised his hand to adjust the radio, and then immediately placed it back on her knee. they bounced along the rutted roads until they made it to the blacktop stretch known in these parts as the highway.

They drove for about twenty minutes when he exited the highway at Warm Springs.

"So, this town of Warm Springs has a population of about twenty thousand. It has a Walmart, a grocery store, a couple of restaurants, and a post office. It also has the hospital."

"Oh, this is where they took you when you had the accident. I thought it looked familiar, but I was in a state of shock and so turned around that night. I just followed the directions your dad gave me and managed to still get here even though I was so worried about you," she said, her voice soft and low.

"It's all good. No worries." He slowed the truck down, looked to the left then proceeded to turn right. "I hope you like Italian." He pulled into one of the parking spots angled in front of the restaurant.

Becca read the words on the plate glass window out loud. "Papa Nona's."

"They have really good food." He jumped out of the truck and made his way over to the passenger side.

"Two," he said, holding up two fingers to the young hostess.

Becca looked around the dimly lit restaurant. Red checkered cloths and a small vase with a single rose adorned each table. When Kyle pulled the chair out for her, she smiled up at him and then sat.

"Tonight's special is angel hair pasta with a Bolognese sauce," the server said, handing them menus. "Care for any wine?"

"Yes, can we have two glasses of your best red wine?" Kyle asked looking at Becca.

"Sure, that sounds lovely."

Over dinner, Becca and Kyle chatted about the purchase of Dickies.

"I really need to find a place to live, though. Do you have any ideas?" She drew the wine glass to her lips and sipped the red contents.

"Are you ready to take on a fixer-upper?"

His warm smile set her skin afire. "Maybe. What do you have in mind?" She brushed her hand along her arm feeling goosebumps.

"I just heard that Spencer's place is going to be auctioned off by the bank. He had no heirs." Kyle lifted his brows then turned his attention to his garden salad with black olives and marinated artichokes.

"That's so sad that he passed away all alone. I wonder what amount we could bid. I have no idea how much of a loan I'd qualify for."

"Loan? Becca," he said, putting his fork down. "This is Steam. You can buy that house outright for twenty thousand cash."

"Twenty thousand dollars? Really?" She twirled the pasta around her fork, using her spoon as a base.

"Maybe even cheaper. Let's go talk to the banker tomorrow. He has all the details." Kyle sipped his wine. "Are you going to make changes to the store?" Kyle spun his pasta around his fork and took a bite.

"Yes, big changes are coming." She smiled broadly.

"Remember, this is little old Steam. We're not used to a lot of changes. Tread lightly." Kyle arched his left brow.

"Well, it's about time Steam gets on board." She laughed at her train euphemism.

Kyle got it too and laughed.

"A second glass of wine, sir?" the server asked.

After two glasses of wine, Becca began to feel a bit warm and cozy inside. Words poured out of her mouth freely. She giggled at all of his jokes and when he reached across the table and cupped her hands, she began to circle his thumbs with hers and then, just as if she'd done it a million times before, she began to play footsie with him under the table. The boots made it difficult though. She finally gave up, and instead ran her hand up his forearm and twirled the hair on his arms. Throbbing, electrifying heat waves pulsed throughout her body.

He leaned over the table, squeezing her hand tightly. "Want to go somewhere quiet?" His low, gravelly voice made her want to leap right out of her chair and kiss his warm, delicious mouth. Instead, she nodded.

A familiar giggle interrupted her amorous thoughts, and she craned her neck to see the source. Standing at the hostess station were Jessica and Robert. Becca's hand flew to her mouth, but she quickly looked back at Kyle.

Kyle's tightly knitted brows told her he didn't have a clue about his dad dating Jessica. Heck, she hadn't either, until recently.

Robert and Kyle locked eyes as they passed the table. Robert and Jessica stopped, smiling ear to ear.

"Hey, you two," Jessica said cheerfully.

"Kyle," Robert said, tipping his head.

Responding offhandedly at first, Kyle softened his reply greeting trying to suppress his surprise..

"We're just stopping in for a bite to eat. Hope you enjoyed your dinner."

"Yes, we had the special. It was delicious," Becca said, trying to smooth the awkward situation.

"Well, have a good evening." Robert stuck his arm out for Jessica.

Jessica looked over her shoulder, smiling as they proceeded to follow the hostess.

Kyle ran his hand over his chin and sighed. "Did you know about that?" He nodded over toward them.

"Well, sort of."

"When were you going to tell me?"

"I didn't know if it was my place to tell you. He's your dad!"

"She's your best friend," he countered, a bit louder.

"Let's go. This is too weird." Becca slid her chair back.

It had grown dark outside while they were eating and Becca had no clue where Kyle was driving. She didn't care, either, because she felt safe with him, and that's all that mattered. He hadn't mentioned his dad or Jessica, so that was a good thing. Talk about a mood killer. He drove up a winding hill and brought the truck to the edge of an overlook then cut the engine.

"Where are we?"

"We used to bring our girlfriends here to make out."

"Ahh. Make Out Lane." She laughed.

He pointed straight ahead. "Those are the lights of Steam."

"Kyle, I know you're upset about your dad and Jessica, but they are grown adults."

"I know, but I just felt like it hit me right in the face. I didn't see it coming."

"They don't really have to tell us. They don't need our permission to date." She snuggled into him, taking his free arm and looping it over her shoulders.

"I guess. How old is she?"

"She's thirty-nine. How old is your dad?"

"He'll be fifty-one."

Becca raised her brows. "They are probably just friends."

"I know Pops is lonely. He's dated some, but I just don't think he's found the one."

"Well, I highly doubt Jessica is the one. It's dinner, that's all. Let's not dwell on them any longer. We didn't come up to Make Out Mountain just to talk," she said, moving slightly out of his hug. She wrapped her arms around his neck.. It might be dark, but she could make out his features, and she knew exactly where that dimple was. She kissed his mouth, and then trailed kisses up and down his neck. He stopped her by lifting her chin, and then devoured her mouth, making them both forget about Robert and Jessica.

Kyle took two steps at a time and landed on the front porch. He'd just reached out to pull the screen door open when he heard a voice.

"Kyle," his dad said.

Kyle looked to the right and saw his father sitting in a rocking chair.

"What's up?" Kyle sat in the chair next to him.

"Are you mad at me?"

Kyle paused a moment before answering. His dad's eyes were easy to read and told him there might be more to this than what Becca thought. "Of course not, Pops. You are free to do what you want." He wasn't quite sure he was convincing enough, so he followed it by adding a bit more. "I think Jessica is a nice girl. You two are having fun."

"Woman, Kyle. She's not a girl," he said in his fatherly tone.

Kyle nodded. "Woman." He began to rock.

"Do you think people will talk about a fifty-year-old dating a thirty-nine-year-old?"

"No, I don't think they'll care. And if they do, just arrest them." He shrugged.

"Ha ha," Robert said.

"Seriously. Date who you want, but just know, Jessica might not stick around here. Becca said she could pick up and move back to New York without a moment's notice."

"Fair enough. I'll proceed with caution."

The two men rocked in silence for a while longer before Kyle spoke. "It's getting serious with Becca."

"You don't say?" Robert chuckled.

"I think I love her."

"Okay, that's big."

"Yup, sure is. She makes my heart feel full. Like I was missing something forever, and here she comes along and fills it up, just like that. I just want to hold her in my arms and kiss her and never let her go."

"That sounds like true love, Son. So, what are you going to do about it?" He stood.

Kyle looked up at his dad. "I'm going to make her fall in love with me so she never wants to leave Steam."

Robert patted Kyle on the shoulder. "Sounds like a plan, Son." He opened the screen door and entered the old farmhouse.

Kyle's phone vibrated and he fished it out of his pocket. It was Becca.

"Hey, girl, did you forget something in my truck?" he teased.

"I'm just lying here on this big old bed thinking about how you'd feel lying next to me, wrapped in my arms … and legs."

He started rocking. "Uh-huh. Well, I can totally get with that. Do you want me to come over?" he teased some more, picturing her in skimpy nightwear.

"Jessica is here, silly. But keep that image for future use, okay?"

"You don't have to worry. I have that image and a lot more. Can I see you tomorrow?"

"Of course, Deputy. You aren't going to get rid of me that easily."

"Glad to hear it. I have something to tell you."

"Oh?"

"Not tonight. Sleep tight and I'll see you tomorrow. Oh, and, Becca?"

"Yes, baby?"

"I'm missing you already."

Becca paused a moment before replying. "I miss you, too. By the way, did you and your dad have a talk?"

"Yes, and I'm okay with them dating. If she makes him happy, that's all that matters."

"Good. But I sure do hope they don't ask to double date!"

They both laughed.

"Good morning," Granddaddy sang out as he poured coffee for both Robert and Kyle.

Both men mumbled in response. Robert immediately picked up the day's newspaper and began to scan the stories. Kyle looked at his phone.

"Okay, you two, who's gonna tell me first?" Granddaddy eased down into the chair, breathing heavily.

Robert glanced over the top of the paper, and then pulled his eyes back down to the print.

"Kyle?" Granddaddy said.

"Tell you what?" Kyle deflected, his eyes not leaving his phone's screen.

"I know you were with the ladies last night. I may be old, but I'm not stupid. Your dad took the longest shower ever and splashed enough cologne on that folks in Warm Springs could smell it. And you, boy, don't tell me you wore your best and darkest jeans, a freshly starched and pressed shirt, and your dating boots for no reason."

Robert folded the paper and laid it on the table. Kyle looked up from his phone.

"Yes, Dad, I went on a date. Had a great dinner with Jessica. And the funny part ... we ran into Kyle and Becca at the restaurant. Are you satisfied now?"

Granddaddy's eyes moved from Robert to Kyle and

then back to Robert. "You're dating Jessica? Becca's friend, Jessica?" He shook his head.

"Granddaddy, this is two thousand and eighteen. It's okay for older men to date younger women." Kyle sighed.

"He's robbing the cradle!"

"She's thirty-nine," Robert said, sliding out his chair with a screech.

"Now, let's simmer down here. Granddaddy, stop it right now. I know Grandmother was a meddler, but you aren't. Leave Pops alone."

Granddaddy sputtered momentarily "You're right. I really was just going to tease him and got carried away. More coffee?" He slid back his chair and crossed over to the kitchen.

Kyle arched his brows and made eye contact with Robert. He shrugged and picked up his phone again. Robert pulled his chair back to the table, unfolded the paper, and finished reading the day's news, while Granddaddy topped off the coffee cups.

Kyle had plans to meet Becca out at the old Spencer ranch later, so he took his own vehicle to the office. Just like he'd told her, the banker said that with an acceptable cash offer the place could be hers.

When he pulled up in front of the sheriff's office, he noticed the patrol car hadn't arrived yet. He unlocked the office, flicked on the lights, and had just powered up his computer when the door open.

"Where'd you go? You left before me."

"I had a stop to make." Robert hung his hat on the rack and proceeded to his desk.

Kyle watched him closely. "I'm going to be taking a long lunch today. Meeting Becca over at Spencer's place." He lowered his head and doodled something on a nearby pad.

"Okay," Robert said, clearly occupied with something.

"What's up, Pops? Everything alright?"

"Yeah, everything is okay." He scratched his head and then reached over to answer the ringing telephone.

Kyle shook his head, chuckling quietly to himself. *Man, he's got it bad.*

"TAKE A RADIO WITH YOU. I'm heading out for lunch, too." Robert opened the door and exited the office.

"Okay. Having lunch with Jessica?" He winked at his dad.

He nodded. "She wants me to help her pick out paint colors for the apartment." He shrugged.

"Tell Mr. Henry over at the hardware store I said hey. I imagine he'll be seeing a lot of me after Becca seals the deal on the old ranch."

Kyle arrived at Spencer's before Becca and began to

look around the old and dilapidated ranch. It had potential but was in serious need of refurbishing. He wondered if Becca had the fortitude to take on such a project. Just then, he heard the sound of tires on gravel and looked up.

Dust billowed everywhere after she came to a complete stop. She popped open the door and hopped out, her eyes sparkling and a wide grin showing all her bright, white teeth.

"Hey, handsome," she said, strolling toward him with her arms wide open.

He leaned in and kissed her cheek, then her mouth.

"So, what do you think?" Her eyes peered over him to the old house.

"It will need a lot of work. Are you ready for the challenge?"

"I don't have much choice. It's not like there are tons of vacant houses or apartments to rent."

"You could share my bedroom. I bet they wouldn't mind." He pulled her in and nuzzled her neck.

She playfully slapped his back. "I care," she said.

"I'm just joking. Shoot, they'd get an earful if you and I—"

"Kyle! Get serious. Let's take a look at the property." She grabbed his hand.

"Be careful. These steps are rickety." He helped her up with caution.

She took out her phone and opened up the Color-Note app. "I'm making a list."

"Put deck, stairs, front door, new siding, upgrade windows, and all trim. And that's just for the exterior. Oh, and paint. Lots of paint and stain." He pulled his lips together tightly and nodded.

"Don't be a pessimist, Kyle."

He shoved the front door open and entered the dark and dusty house. "All new subfloor, carpet or wood, baseboards, update kitchen to include cabinetry and countertops, and paint," he rattled off.

She followed him down the hallway.

With half of his body in the bathroom, he examined the space. "New tiles, new shower surround, and update cabinets and sink … and paint."

She followed him to the bedrooms.

"Just paint and flooring."

"So, how much do you think these renovations will cost me?"

Digging his hands deep inside his pockets he rocked back on his heels calculating the cost and amount of work to be done. She followed closely behind him.

He rubbed his hand across his chin then ran his fingers through his hair. "I'd say close to fifty thousand."

"Fifty thousand!"

"That's not counting some landscaping."

She lowered her head while shaking it. "I don't know. That's a lot of money."

"How much are you going to offer for the place?" he spoke softly and steady.

"I was going to make an offer of twenty thousand or so. I mean that's what you said. And the banker said it was an acceptable offer."

He flicked his tongue, making clicking sounds as he walked around the living room. "I think you should offer fifteen thousand to the bank. They'll still be making a profit. This house has been paid for a zillion times over. They're just recouping some administrative costs. It really is ninety-nine-point nine percent profit for them."

"Okay." Her face lit up and made him smile.

"We'll try to cut some costs in repairing this old place. I think you'll love living out here."

"I do too, especially if you're here."

"I'm not going anywhere." He stepped closer to her and took her hands. "I've wanted to tell you something for a while. Last night really brought it home for me. I think I'm …" She reached for his hands and held them tightly. His heart began to beat fast, and he wondered if he'd find the courage to tell her how he really felt.

"If you're going to say you're falling in love with me, I feel the same way about you." She batted her lashes at him, and it took everything he had and more not to take her on the old rotted and dirty floors right then.

"I haven't felt this way in a long time. I think about you every minute of the day."

She arched her brows and nodded. "I think about you, too. I know it's crazy. We've only known each other a short while, but I guess if it's right, it's right, huh?" She lifted her shoulders and then dropped them.

"I guess so, baby." He pulled her close, staring into her blue eyes, wondering if this could really be happening.

"I love you, Kyle," she said, her eyes never wavering from his.

He leaned in and kissed her. She wrapped her arms around his neck and held him tightly. They fit like a glove, and all he could think about was her dainty little frame wrapped up in his strong arms and what she'd feel like flesh to flesh.

After a few moments of intense kissing, they separated. "I didn't get to finish saying what I was going to say." He ran his strong, big hands up her arms. "I love you, Rebecca Parsons." His eyes twinkled in the sunlight that seeped through the window.

"Oh, Kyle," she said, cupping his face. "I've waited a long time to hear those words."

"I don't say them lightly, Becca. I mean them. I'm going to love you from morning to night if you'll let me." His eyes grew misty, and he had to fight back the tears.

"Kyle, that's so sweet of you. I hope I'm worthy of your love." She blinked back a few tears her own, hoping it made him feel a bit better about his own misty eyes.

He kissed the top of her head before taking a step back and grabbed her hands, playfully swinging them to and fro. "Do you ever think about marriage?" He didn't know where those words came from. They just slipped out, and now there was no way of getting them back. He squeezed her hands.

She shook her head a few times.

His eyes grew big. "Oh, I guess I shouldn't have been so quick to assume." He let go of her hands.

"Kyle." She picked up his hands and held them, circling his thumbs with hers. "I just meant … I never thought about it before. Not until you."

His eyes zoomed right in on her coy smile and the way she moistened her dry lips with the tip of her tongue. The hair on the back of his neck began to prickle, and he felt his pulse quicken through every vein in his body.

He pulled her close and kissed her, as a small breathless whisper escaped her lips. "I love you."

He picked her up and twirled her around. "I love you, too."

After they kissed and teased one another, Kyle had another surprise up his sleeve, and after a little more kissing and teasing, he drove her back to the hotel to change. While she was in the bathroom, he flipped through channels on the television, but he couldn't concentrate. Knowing she was just on the other side of the wall in lacy panties and a matching bra about drove him insane. He wondered what she'd do if he just busted open the door. He stood. Then he sat back down. After a quick second he stood again then quickly sat back down. He was getting up again when she came out.

"Okay, dressed in jeans, T-shirt, and boots." She twirled around to show off her duds.

"You look great. Let's go." He jumped off the bed and tossed on his hat.

"Where are we going?"

"It's a surprise."

She drew her lips up in a tight twist and knitted her brows. "I gathered that, Kyle Huntsman."

After a rather short ride on bumpy back roads he pulled up to a barn where another truck was parked. She glanced around and noticed horses. She tore her eyes away from the horses and smiled. "Are we going horseback riding?"

He nodded. "You'll need this."

She took the cream-colored cowboy hat he passed to her and put it on her head. "How do I look?"

"Like a million bucks." He leaned in and waited for her to meet him. Their lips brushed softly, and then she pressed harder for a more passionate kiss. He aimed to please her, so he obliged and gave her a nice titillating kiss that left her begging for more.

"Oh, wow. Now that's a kiss."

"There's more where that came from." He popped open the truck door and hopped out, rushing to meet her at the other side to help her out of the truck.

"Hey there, Kyle," a jolly man said as he emerged from the barn. He shook Kyle's hand.,.

"Hey, Mr. Phipps. This is my girlfriend, Becca." He moved her forward by placing his hand on her back.

"Hi, Mr. Phipps," she said, shaking his hand.

"Here to ride the horses?" He smiled exposing a few missing teeth.

Becca nodded. "I guess so. He surprised me."

"Have you ever ridden before?"

"No, never. Unless the ponies at the fair count."

"Don't worry, hon. Mr. Phipps has some of the nicest horses around. That's why I brought you out here. We have two horses back at our place, but they are for the more experienced rider. You get good at it, and we can take ours out." He smiled over at Mr. Phipps.

"I have two already saddled and ready to go." Mr. Phipps walked over to the gate and unhitched it. There, standing tied up, were two horses. "This mare is as sweet as honey."

"What's her name?" Becca asked.

"Honey." The old man chuckled.

"And for you, Kyle, this is Magic. He's a senior citizen but don't let that fool you. He'll still give you a great ride."

"Is Honey a senior citizen as well?" Becca stuck her foot in the stirrup and Kyle with both hands on her bottom gave her a boost.

"Yes, all my horses are seniors. They make great first horse riding experiences, especially for children. I get kids from Warm Springs all the time," Mr. Phipps added as he shut the gate behind them.

Kyle pulled out his pocket watch. "Okay, so we'll be back in about two hours, give or take."

"Sounds good. I might be gone when you get back."

"No worries. I'll take their saddles off, wipe them down, and make sure they're secured behind the fence."

"Thanks, Kyle." Mr. Phipps palmed a wave then jumped in his truck.

The two trotted side by side for about an hour when he asked her if she wanted to stop. She hated to admit it, but her butt and thighs were crying out for some rest. He found a nice shady place with a small stream running by. While the horses drank from the stream, they sat on a blanket he'd brought. At first, they talked about the horse ride. Then he tossed a few pebbles into the stream. But when she laced her arm with his and pulled him close, all he really wanted to do was kiss every inch of her. And so, he did.

While leaning over her, he pushed some of her golden locks away from her face. She watched his every movement. When she touched him, his heart began to beat, and just like some well-oiled machine, he leaned in to kiss her lips. It was automatic.

She clung to his neck as he kissed her, and when he could feel her moving under him, and things were getting a bit too hot for even him, he stopped her. "If you don't stop moving like that, I'll just have to do something about it," he said with a low, sexy growl. She moved her hips under him again.

He threw his head back and sighed. When he came back down into position, he smiled, showing the cute dimples she was absolutely crazy about. Then he kissed her hard, dipping his tongue in the space between her lips as she opened them for him. He tasted her tentatively and with fervor, which only made her writhe under his weight. He groaned then rolled her over on top, taking his place below her.

She nuzzled his neck as he dipped his fingers inside her waistband, seeking the heat that tried to consume her. The low moaning coming from her lips intensified the mood. He rolled her back over, and while she watched, he tossed off his shirt and unbuttoned his jeans, sending her into a frenzy he wasn't sure he'd be able to control. But he would try.

"Kyle," she whispered as they held each other close.

"Becca, damn, I can't get enough of you."

Her mouth was so warm, the caress of her lips softer than he could have ever imagined. The outdoors seemed to increase their pleasure, and he was thankful they were out in the middle of nowhere.

Afterwards, they held each other and just listened to the sounds of nature.

"Kyle," she mumbled with her eyes half closed.

"Yeah," he replied in a sluggish tone.

"I really like horseback riding. Will you take me again?"

Just then he rolled up on his side, resting on his elbow. "You're bad." He quickly kissed her.

"Bad as in bad, or bad as in good?" She snickered.

"Either way, I'm definitely taking you horseback riding again."

CHAPTER 17

Becca and Jessica sat in heavy, wooden arm chairs directly across from the president of the small bank who approved their business loan. It was a big day for them.

Becca would sign and initial documents and then pass them over to Jessica. They laughed and joked how their hands and wrists were getting tired from all the signing.

"So, have you decided on a new name for the drugstore?" The banker looked at them over the top of his dark rimmed reading glasses.

"Not yet. We've had a few ideas." Becca smiled at the grey-haired man dressed in a dark suit.

"Rebecca, I've heard back from the board. They decided to accept your offer of fifteen thousand dollars on the Spencer ranch."

"Oh, that's fantastic!" she said, lowering her head and initialing away.

"There's just one catch."

She raised her head quickly and stared at the man. "Oh?"

"It has to be cash."

She leaned back and crossed her arms. "Cash?"

He nodded. "It's such a small amount, they don't want it to be financed."

"I'm using a lot of my cash for the business. There was the down payment, closing costs, and fees." She looked up at Kyle who was standing quietly nearby.

"How much do you have?" the banker asked.

She drew in a deep breath. "Probably about half."

The man rapped the desk with his fingers. "Well, see if you can come up with the rest. That house isn't going anywhere. I doubt anyone will buy it."

"It's just so disappointing."

"You can say that again," Jessica added.

Becca shot her a wild look. "Why?"

"Cuz that means we have to share the apartment."

Becca furrowed her brows. "Like I want to do that."

"Well, I think that's the last of the signing," Jessica said, pushing the last document toward the banker.

He pushed his chair back and stood. "Thank you for your business. Good luck on the store. I'll stop by for lunch sometime." He extended his hand.

Becca, Jessica, and Kyle walked out of the bank with

keys and smiles. But deep down, Becca was sad. She wasn't going to get the ranch like she wanted.

"Robert and I already picked out the paint colors. So if you have to move in with me, just know, I've already started the decorating process." Jessica lowered her chin and gave Becca that don't mess with me look.

Becca shrugged it off. "No worries. I don't plan on staying there long. I have to think of something so I can get that house."

Kyle slung his arm over her shoulders. "We'll think of something."

OVER THE NEXT couple of weeks, the drugstore went through a total transformation. While Jessica put the finishing touches on the apartment, Becca and Kyle got the store ready. They installed laminate flooring, painted shelves, installed new countertops in a white quartz with turquoise specks for the lunch counter, and had the stools reupholstered in a turquoise vinyl to match. Kyle installed some new lighting, and Becca replaced the antique cash register with a newer model and took the old one over to Andy Taylor's shop to have him sell it.

Over coffee, Becca ran through the new menu ideas with Kyle.

"I like that you kept most of the favorites and just

added a few new ones. Most people order burgers, fries, and shakes there."

"That's what we thought, too. So, we just added a few new versions of the regular cheeseburger, like avocado and bacon, and the barbecue and bacon should also be a hit here."

"Corn chip pie?"

"Yes, that's where we start with a layer of corn chips, ladle on homemade chili, and top it with diced onions, shredded cheese, and a dollop of sour cream." Becca's mouth watered talking about one of her childhood favorites.

Kyle rubbed his stomach. "You're making me hungry."

"Let's go have lunch then." Becca hopped off the chrome stool.

"Where's Jessica?" Kyle's eyes travelled to the back door where the stairs leading to the apartment were.

"She and your dad are looking over swatches or something." She laughed.

"Yeah, I bet they are." He shook his head.

"So, have you girls decided on a name for the place?" Kyle held her hand as they walked to the truck.

"Yep, we have. I'm surprised you hadn't heard yet … you know, with loose lips, Jessica and your dad, and all." She giggled.

"He's getting in late, and not talking much. Granddaddy and I made a pact that we won't ask him anything. We'll just be ready to catch him if he falls."

"Do you think he'll be able to recover if Jessica breaks his heart?" She clicked her seat belt and tugged at it to tighten it.

"I don't know, Becca. He's falling for her pretty hard. I hope she's not just messing with him." He started the engine.

"It will make it really hard to live and work here if they have a falling out. I'm going to talk to her, but like you and Granddaddy, I'm treading lightly."

Kyle looked over his shoulder and then backed out. He drove toward the diner at the far end of town, next to the hotel where the girls had been living. Once inside, they ordered lunch and talked casually about how their lives had changed.

"You never did finish telling me what you are going to name the drugstore." He dug into his blue plate special of fried chicken, okra, and mashed potatoes.

She clasped her hands and rested them on the table. "We had several contenders, but when it was all said and done, only one name really fit the place, the town, and the image we're trying to portray."

He set his fork down.

"Full Steam Ahead Grill & Shop."

"That's perfect, Becca!"

"We even had the sign maker design an old steamer train for the sign."

"Okay, so the next order of business is the ranch." He chewed a bite of the mashed potatoes.

"I've racked my brain and scraped every penny, but I'm still about ten thousand dollars short."

Kyle reached into his shirt pocket and pulled out a folded piece of paper. He slid it across the table.

Becca's eyes locked onto it. "What's this?"

He tipped his head. "Open it."

Pulling the paper closer, she unfolded it and read silently. "Kyle …" she gasped.

"Congratulations, baby. You're the proud owner of the old Spencer ranch." He slid out his side of the booth and slid in with her, playfully nudging her shoulder with his.

"Kyle Huntsman, you shouldn't have. I mean, how did you?" A tear rolled down her cheek.

"Well, Granddaddy didn't want a fuss to be made over it, but he fronted the money for the house."

"Well, I need to pay him back. I promise I'll work hard, and every extra cent I make off the store and grill will go to repay him." She spoke fast and could feel her heart beating a mile a minute.

Kyle took her hands and held them. "That's not necessary. See … he said it's a gift."

Becca first focused on his gorgeous brown eyes, then her eyes travelled past his dimple to his full lips. She flashed a smile that was both warm and inviting but with a hint of uncertainty. A gift?" She shook her head. "I don't understand. What sort of gift?"

"A wedding gift."

Becca's hand flew to her mouth as she watched Kyle pull a small dark blue velvet box out of his pocket.

"I didn't want to do it here, like this, but ..." He popped open the box.

Becca marveled at the glistening white gold band with a princess cut diamond. "I love you, Kyle," she said, brushing the tears away as quickly as they rolled down her cheeks.

He took the ring out of the box and slid it on her finger. "Will you be my wife, Rebecca Parsons?"

She brought her hand to her chest and tilted her head slightly. "Yes. Yes, I will."

CHAPTER 18

"Congratulations, Son," Robert said, shaking his hand and then pulling him in for a hug.

"I can't believe she said yes," Kyle said, clearly emotional.

"What do you mean, you can't believe she said yes?" Granddaddy joked. "You're the most eligible bachelor in Steam, and a mighty fine one at that."

Robert cut his eyes toward his dad.

"Young, eligible bachelor." Granddaddy corrected then left the room, grumbling under his breath.

"Seriously, Son. I'm very happy for you. When's the wedding?"

"We didn't talk about a date. I just gave her the ring while we were having lunch."

"Does she have family?"

Kyle knitted his brows.

"You know, a mom, dad, brothers or sisters?"

"We never really talked about her family. I guess there's a lot I still don't know about her." His voice became almost a whisper.

Robert hated the sound of defeat in Kyle's voice. He reached over and patted him on the shoulder and then walked away.

"Hey, honey. What's going on?" He paced his small room with the phone to his ear.

"I'm just getting ready to drive over to Warm Springs with Jessica. We heard they have a furniture store."

"Yeah, they do. If they don't have it, they can get it from Dallas."

"That's good to know. What's wrong? I sense something is wrong. Did you change your mind about marrying me?"

Kyle stopped pacing. "No, of course not!"

"Okay, then. Is your dad okay? Your granddaddy?"

"Yeah, they are all just fine. But, Becca?"

"Yes?"

"You've never mentioned your family to me."

There was a great pause of silence between them. "Well, let's see. My parents are divorced, and Mom lives in New Jersey with her third, or is it fourth husband? I don't know. I lost track after husband number two. My dad, the last I heard, was living in California, but that could have changed as well. I haven't spoken to him in four years. And my brother, Peter … he lives in Canada. I think he lives in Canada. I don't really know anymore. I guess you could say I'm an orphan." She laughed.

"I just wondered if your family would want to come to the wedding." Kyle held his breath.

"As I said, I wouldn't be able to get in touch with anyone but my mother. I'll definitely let her know, but Kyle … there's no real relationship between my mother and me. We let that ship sail a long time ago. I think it was after—"

Kyle interrupted her. "Husband number two?"

"Yeah, probably," she whispered.

"Well, I won't keep you from your girl outing. Have fun at Warm Springs. Can we have dinner tonight?"

"I told Jessica we'd grab sushi before heading home. We're both craving it bad." She giggled.

"Okay. Call me when you get back so I don't worry about you pretty single ladies loose among the prying eyes of cowboys."

"Love you," she said, ending the conversation.

"Love you, too."

Kyle tucked his khaki uniform shirt into his snug jeans and pinned on his badge. On his way out the door, he grabbed his hat.

He drove out to the Spencer ranch where he met a group of young mean ready to work. They had a lot of ground to cover in a few short hours, and he wasted no time getting to the instructions.

"So, the porch needs a total gutting. I have wood scheduled to be delivered in two hours. In the main area of the house, I need all cabinetry removed, and several pieces of subfloor have to be replaced in the living room. He must have had a water leak. So, if we can get the demolition going, that will be a big plus. My fiancée won't be around at all today."

Two big guys grabbed the pickaxes that leaned up against the truck and began to tear the rotted porch and stairs apart. Meanwhile, some other guys started ripping the cabinets out of the kitchen. In no time the men were hurling rotted wood left and right and Kyle moved out of the way in fear of getting hit by flying debris..

"I have to get back to the office, but you have my number. Call me if you have any questions. If you can get the porch done today, that would be great. Be back tomorrow at the same time." He nodded to the foreman of the crew and then got into his truck. By the time he looked in his rearview mirror, the front porch was all but a pile of rotted wood. A wide smile spread across his face. He couldn't wait for his baby girl to see this.

"How's it going out at the ranch?" Robert asked.

"Man, those guys are aggressive. In the twenty

minutes I stood there, they completely dismantled the porch, and cabinets came flying out the back door!"

"Yeah, those guys know how to demo." Robert looked away.

"I figure the porch will be done by this evening. Then I have Tim coming to paint the walls. After that, we can get the tile laid in the bathrooms and kitchen and be ready for the new cabinets and countertops. The last thing going in is the hardwood, carpet, and baseboards."

"How are you going to keep her busy each and every day so she won't know what you're up to?" Robert caught Kyle's gaze.

"That's where you come in. I need you to ask Jessica to help us."

Robert tipped his forehead. "I don't see her until tomorrow."

"Can't you call her?"

Robert picked up the phone and dialed her number, and Kyle listened in as his dad asked Jessica for her help. It seemed like a done deal.

"She suggested maybe they'd get drunk and spend the night at Warm Springs." Robert shrugged.

"Get drunk and spend the night? That's an awful plan, Pops!"

"Well, not much else to do between here and Warm Springs, unless you want them to drive to Dallas?"

Kyle drew in a deep breath. "No, that's gonna have to do. Wait, I know. I can take her to Dallas. I'll book us a hotel right now." His eyes lit up as he searched for the number of the hotel he wanted to take her to.

Around midday, Becca contacted Kyle to let him know that their plans had changed slightly. He played along, never giving her any reason to think that he'd been behind the extended overnight stay in Warm Springs.

"Hey, I was wondering. How'd you like to go to Dallas with me?"

"Ooh, that sounds nice. When?"

"I thought I'd pick you up at the hotel in Warm Springs, and we can go from there."

"But I don't have any clothes. Jessica just dumped this overnight thing on me as it is. I'm going to be re-wearing today's clothes. I need to come back and pack a few things."

"Okay. I'll pick you up from the hotel at around noon, then."

"Did she buy it?" Robert leaned back in his office chair with his arms crossed.

"Yeah, I think so. At least, I hope so." Kyle leaned back in his chair with arms crossed and stared out into space.

"What did he want?" Jessica ran her hand along the couch back and flashed a smile at Becca.

"He wants to take me to Dallas tomorrow."

"Dallas?"

"Yeah. Said we'd go shopping for house items and have dinner out."

Jessica plopped down in a rocker recliner. "That's strange. Why the sudden idea to go to Dallas, I wonder?" The ever-quizzical journalist in her replied.

Becca sat in another chair nearby. "I'm not really sure, but I've wanted to check out Dallas again, so that's fine with me. This chair is comfy."

The women inspected every inch of the furniture store, and Jessica purchased a couple of things before they moved on to the big-box store for some essentials. After an exhausting shopping day, they settled into the one and only sushi restaurant in a hundred-mile radius.

Becca stirred the wasabi paste with her chopsticks, added soy sauce and then plunged a piece of the roll into the mixture and popped it into her mouth. "This is pretty good." She tipped her head toward the plates of cut rolls.

Jessica raised her hand to get the server's attention. "Two more cocktails, please."

After two rolls and four cocktails each, the girls headed to the hotel. Tired, full, and a bit tipsy, they soon fell into bed. But not before they talked about their new adventure in Steam.

"Do you think I'm crazy for dating Robert?" Jessica said almost asleep.

"No. I mean age is just a number, right?"

"He's very romantic in an old-school sort of way," Jessica responded.

"Well, that makes sense." Becca giggled.

"I mean, he's a gentleman. That's not something we see every day in the city," Jessica said.

"Why do you think I'm in love with Kyle? He may not be old, but he's got that old-school sort of charm, too." She rolled over to her side and propped her body up on her elbow. "It's a total turn-on."

"Tell me about it. I can hardly resist Robert."

Becca knitted her brow, concerned she'd learn too much information. Information she'd never be able to erase from her brain. "Yeah, don't say any more about your relationship with Robert. It could get kind of … well … yucky. I don't want to have to hide anything from Kyle." She rolled onto her back and stared at the ceiling.

"I get it. It's hard for a grown adult to see his father having fun and sex."

"Jessica! What part of don't tell me anymore, don't you understand?" She gasped. "Good night." She rose up, turning off the light then plopped back down, sliding under the covers.

"Oh, please! You two need to get a life." Jessica turned off her light.

CHAPTER 20

Kyle pulled out his old pocket watch, and contemplated how much time he had. He had to make a quick stop at the ranch to see the progress and then get to the hotel to pick up Becca before she suspected anything.

Dropping his jaw in utter surprise, Kyle jumped out of the truck. He spotted the foreman and made a beeline to him. "Wow, I'm impressed. The front porch looks fantastic. What did you guys do, work until midnight?"

"Nah, this is what can be accomplished when you offer up a keg of beer." He roared a deep, hearty belly laugh.

"Well, if that's what makes them work good and fast, I'll throw a keg in, too."

"Come on inside," the foreman said, leading the way.

Once inside, Kyle could see that this crew meant business. The kitchen and baths were gutted; all the old carpet and linoleum removed, and the subfloor in the living room had been replaced.

"What's left to do?" Kyle asked, peering into each room and moving on to the next.

The foreman looked over his clipboard. "The windows are going in later today, and then we'll tackle the dry rot repair on the siding and paint. The inside is ready for whatever you have planned next." He raised his eyes to meet Kyle's.

"Okay, I'll get everything else lined up. Thanks a lot." He held out his hand to the foreman.

"No worries. Glad we were able to help."

"I gotta run. I'll be by in a couple of days to see how the rest looks, and I'll write you a check then."

"Sounds good."

Kyle hit the road, and flew to the hotel to get Becca.

"Why are you so out of breath?" Becca asked as she grabbed her purse.

"Oh, just trying to finish up some loose ends. The time got away from me." He reached for her bags from her shopping spree. He helped her into the truck and tossed her bags in the back seat. "Before you buckle up …" He leaned over.

She leaned in and met him halfway.

❧

He drove her back to her hotel room in Steam so she could pack an overnight bag and change her clothes. Once she was ready, he helped her back in the truck.

"You look beautiful today." He leaned forward and kissed her.

She moved away after the kiss. "You look pretty handsome yourself." She winked.

"Ready for Dallas?" He started the engine and put it in gear.

"I am. I've been ready for a while." She buckled her belt and pulled it tight.

"Here we go," he said, smiling ear to ear.

"I've had a total blast today. My feet are so tired with all the shopping. You're one heck of a guy to let me pull you along into all those stores," she said, clasping hands on the table at the restaurant.

Her eyes danced in the candlelight, melting his heart, and he how he could be so lucky to have her in his life, making him feel whole.

"I love you, Becca."

"I love you, too," she said, squeezing his hands.

"No, that's why I let you pull me into all those stores —because I love you."

She tossed her head back and laughed, sparking a deep arousal in him that he couldn't explain.

"We haven't set a date for the wedding," he said.

"I've been thinking about that. What sort of wedding do you want?"

"A church wedding, of course." He blinked.

"Oh, okay. It's good we're talking about it now. I've always wanted an outdoor wedding."

"How about we compromise?" He let go of her hands and took a sip of his bourbon. "We get married in the church and have the reception outdoors?"

"Okay, but how's that a compromise?" She held the cocktail glass to her lips and then drew in a taste.

"We could have the wedding and the reception at the church. There's a back room for socials. The ladies in town love to have potlucks."

She tipped her head. "Oh, I see. Well, I'm not a potluck kind of lady."

"Not yet." His eyes twinkled.

KYLE RESTED his head against the headboard and waited for her to come out of the bathroom. The anticipation of seeing her was almost too much. Talk about performance anxiety.

She waltzed out of the changing area adjacent to the bathroom wearing a short pastel pink silk kimono, and as she approached the bed, she untied it, exposing matching boxer shorts and a camisole. He had to restrain his desire to pull her right on top of him, and it grew increasingly more difficult, the closer she came toward the bed.

He drew in a deep breath, held it for a second, and then exhaled. "God, you are beautiful," he said, motioning toward her with open arms.

She let the robe drop to the floor and climbed into his arms, snuggling in the crux of his strong hold. His heart jumped and soared.

She looked up at him with her baby blues, and that was the final straw. He pulled her up so she was on top of him. Her hair dangled down, tickling his face as she positioned herself. Then in a hungry passion, their mouths touched, and everything he'd held back unraveled in a second. There was no way any of it would be contained again. Ever.

OVER ORANGE JUICE, coffee, fresh fruit, and muffins, the two lovebirds dined while still in bed.

"I could get used to this," she said, stirring the cream into her coffee.

"You mean you don't just long to be settled into your new ranch house in Steam?" His eyes flirted with her, and he knew that could mean trouble.

"I'm getting used to the idea." She looped her arm with his.

"I have to make a phone call. I'll be right back." He

loosened her hold and slid out from under the covers, careful not to tip over the lap tray.

Becca shrugged in confusion, and then popped a strawberry into her mouth.

He rummaged through his pockets and retrieved his phone, holding it up for her to see. "I'll just be a minute." He ducked into the bathroom.

He got all the updated details about the ranch. Seemed things were moving at a fast pace—faster than expected. He made a few more phone calls then headed back out to the main room.

He put on the brakes when he got a look at her, sprawled out on top of the covers, holding a strawberry to her ever-sexy mouth. He tossed the phone in the direction of the chair and leapt onto the bed, grabbing her.

"What took you so long?" she said coyly.

He shook his head and grunted then he nuzzled and trailed wet kisses up her neck. She pushed him away, tempting him with the dangling strawberry. He played like he was going to eat it, and then at the last minute, he devoured her instead. The only breakfast in bed he had in mind was a blue-eyed New Yorker that pulled his heartstrings.

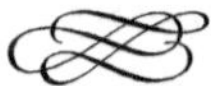

CHAPTER 21

Keeping her busy and distracted proved to be harder than he expected. Thankfully, she was knee-deep in getting Full Steam Ahead Grill up and operational. The work at the ranch was almost complete. Kyle, Robert, and even Granddaddy were putting the finishing touches on it.

"This doesn't even look like the same place," Robert said, shaking his head.

"I know, right?" Kyle opened another bag of mulch and spread it in the new flower bed. "Granddaddy, you did a great job planting these lavender plants. I hope your knees will forgive you." Kyle smiled as he helped him up from the cushiony knee pad.

"Heating pad, aspirin, and a stiff drink will make it all worth it." Granddaddy stretched his arms and his legs, letting a little grunt escape his mouth.

Kyle peered at his pocket watch. "I need to go get her." He rubbed his hands in anticipation of seeing her face.

"Okay, we'll be inside with the air-conditioning running. Hurry on back," Robert said, shooing him away.

Kyle stopped at the truck and watched as his dad and granddaddy took the stairs to the porch. "Hey," he called out.

The two men turned around.

"Thank you," he hollered.

Both men smiled and then, turning toward the door, put their arms around each other.

Kyle sighed then jumped inside the truck and took off for the Grill.

When he entered the Grill, he found Jessica on her tiptoes stocking shelves.

"Where's Becca?"

"Oh, geez, Kyle, you scared me," she shrieked.

"Sorry. Where's Becca?"

"She's in the kitchen, I think."

Kyle crossed over to the luncheon counter and rang the little bell. Out came Becca, wiping her hands on a towel. Her eyes lit up when she saw him sitting on the stool.

"What brings you in here today?"

"You," he said in a low, sexy tone.

"Well, then. You came to the right place." She play-swatted him on the hands with the towel.

"Don't do that, girl. That right there is too sexy for in here." He shook his head.

"Seriously, what's up?" She tried to lessen the sexual tension, if only for a moment.

"Can you take a ride with me?" he asked, his voice steady and calm.

"WHERE ARE WE GOING?" She looked out the window as he drove.

"You'll see." He drove a bit then pulled onto the familiar road.

"The ranch?" She pulled her head from the window and studied him. "Your dad is here," she said pointing to the sheriff's car.

"Yup," is all he said.

"What's going on, Kyle? Wait. This can't be. What happened?" She jumped out of the truck as soon as it came to a complete stop. She whirled around to face him while walking backwards. "Kyle Huntsman, what have you done? This place looks fabulous." She turned back around, staring at the place. "Oh, look, landscaped beds with lavender. And the house paint. I love the color. Oh my God! The porch." She ran up the stairs and proceeded to walk the length of the porch. She grabbed on the railing and stretched her head out from under the roofline. "The view from here is wonderful."

He joined her on the porch and pulled her in close. "I did this for you. Because I love you, and I want you to be happy here with me. I know it's a big move, coming from a big city like New York. You'll make me the happiest man on earth and in Steam by marrying me, loving me, and taking me with all my faults."

"Faults? You don't have any, Kyle. I'm the one who came here thinking I was too good for Steam. You taught me how to be humble, thankful for the small things, and I'll forever love you and hold you dear to my heart. I don't know if I'm worthy of all this …" She looked around. "But I'm going to give it my all, of that you can be sure of." She laid her head on his chest.

"There's more. Come inside." He took her hand.

"Surprise," Granddaddy and Robert yelled.

Becca covered her mouth to muffle her sounds of joy, but she couldn't stop the tears from falling nonstop down her face.

Granddaddy and Robert circled her with their arms. "Welcome home, Becca," they said in unison.

Becca shook her head frantically while crying. "I can't believe you all did this for me."

Kyle pulled her into the kitchen.

She ran her hand along the granite countertops. "Beautiful," she said, choking back tears.

He grabbed her hand and led her down the hall toward the bathrooms and bedrooms. Each room surprised her more than the last. After they toured the rest of the house, they made their way back to the living room.

"This is where we should have the reception, Kyle," she blurted.

"That's a great idea, baby." He circled her waist and held her. "So you like everything?" He studied her face for a reaction.

"I love it. Not as much as I love you, but I definitely love it." She stepped closer into his arms. "I'll never be able to top this."

THE LAST FEW days had been an accumulation of whirlwind events. Even young Kyle was feeling the exhaustion from going and doing. The grand opening of the Grill, scheduled for a week from Saturday, gave them just enough breathing room for a little break—a much needed break, but not a break from each other. No, that would never fly, especially after the words she'd whispered to him. His heart jumped several beats just thinking about all she wanted to do to him. He wiped the grin off his face as he dressed for a quiet evening with Becca,. Robert was over at Jessica's new apartment, decorating. *Yeah, right.* And Granddaddy was nursing his sore body from the gardening he'd done. So just Kyle and Becca cozy on the couch, watching reruns of *Longmire* with only a bowl of popcorn between them, seemed like the perfect date.

"Are you ready for the grand opening?" He tossed up a piece of popcorn and caught it in his mouth.

"As ready as I'll be. Shelves are stocked, the menu is completed, and the …" Her hand flew over her mouth.

"What's wrong?" His eyes widened at her gasp.

"I don't have a short-order cook!" A tear rolled down her face.

"How'd we forget that?" A puzzled look appeared on Kyle's face.

"I don't know." She stood and paced the dimly lit living room. "I guess I got so caught up in other things."

"Okay, let me think. Who could we get?" he said.

CHAPTER 22

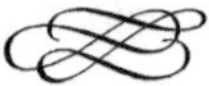

They watched as Dirk tied the white apron around his waist. He knew his way around a kitchen, that was for sure. He began to brown the meat for the chili and got things going. Satisfied he had it under control, the two stepped out of his way.

"I think your granddaddy is going to work out just fine. And since we're only open for lunch, he can still work in his garden or whatever else he wants to do. And working part-time here won't affect his Social Security check." Becca reached for Kyle's hands.

She liked the way his hands felt in hers, but truthfully, she liked the way they felt all over her body. She trembled slightly thinking about all his smooth moves in the bedroom.

"Yup, it's going to work out just great. So where's your sidekick today?" He winked.

She knew he was teasing her. He knew full well where Jessica was. "Those two can't keep their hands off of each other," she said, taking his hand and leading him toward the front of the store.

"Too much information," he groaned with a pained look on his face.

"I know, sorry." She kissed him on the cheek. "But we're going to have to get used to it. What are we going to do if he moves into the apartment with her?" She bit her bottom lip and grimaced.

"That would never happen. I can't see him leaving Granddaddy all alone. Now, maybe she'd move in there with them." He arched his brows then leaned over and grabbed a roll of mints. "Can you put these on my tab?"

"Tab? What do you think this is?" She playfully grabbed it out of his hand. "Why do you need this?" She twisted her shoulders to and fro and batted her lashes.

He looked over his shoulder and when he realized no one was looking, he slipped his hands around her waist, pulling her in for a kiss.

She didn't care if the store was full of shoppers. This man was hard to resist. She lovingly kissed him back.

"More where that came from later. I gotta get back to the office." He winked.

She sighed then she perked up. He totally got her heart pumping. "Okay. Come back at lunchtime. Dirk will love that you came out on his first day."

"Are you kidding? Dad, me, Andy, and Krisi … we are all coming by for lunch."

"Krisi?" She furrowed her brows.

"Now, Becca Parsons, I do believe you're jealous." He leaned in for one more kiss. He shook his head. "Got to go," he said, touching his mouth and stumbling out of the store.

NOT AN OPEN STOOL could be found during Dirk's inaugural lunch shift. Seems that the corn chip pie was very popular as well as the thick frosty shakes. While discussing their first day's success with Jessica, Becca felt her phone vibrate in her pocket. "I've got to take this," she said as she walked away.

"Hello, Mother. How are you?"

"Hey, dear. I'm just calling to see how you are."

"I'm doing well. Jessica and I got the store and grill opened, and my house is fully remodeled thanks to my honey, Kyle. I'm all moved in and loving it. We're busy planning the wedding, too. Are you still going to come?" She paused.

"Yeah, sure, hon. I wouldn't miss it. I just wanted to let you know, I haven't been able to locate your dad or brother yet."

Becca stared out the window and counted to three. "That's okay. Thanks for trying."

"I'm not giving up. I just wanted to let you know that as of now, I haven't had any luck. Hey, why couldn't your police boyfriend find them? Don't they find missing people?"

"First of all, he's a deputy sheriff. And second of all, I haven't asked him."

"Okay, hon. I can hear the stress in your voice. Let me know if I can help you with anything."

"Yeah, cuz you have so much experience with weddings." Becca's sarcasm travelled through the receiver.

"I'm gonna ignore that little snide comment," her mother said.

"Sorry, Mom. It's just been sort of stressful around here. But things are finally smoothing out, and I can concentrate on the wedding. I'll email details over to you soon. I gotta run."

"I love you, Becca."

Becca paused, trying to control her emotions. She finally squeaked out the three little words, although she wasn't sure she really meant them, nor was she convinced that her mother believed them.

AFTER A LONG DAY on her feet, all she dreamed about was a hot bath with lavender. She crawled out of her clothes and placed her toes in the water to test the heat.

Satisfied it was perfect, she slipped down into the warm water and breathed in the smell she loved so dearly. She closed her eyes and relaxed, letting her bones enjoy the warm water. Her phone started dancing all over the closed toilet lid.

"Damn. Can't a girl take a bath without interruptions?" She sat up and pulling the towel from the towel bar, dried off her hand, and reached for the phone. It was Kyle.

"Hey," she said, leaning back into the tub, taking care not to get her phone wet.

"What are you doing?"

"Soaking in a bath."

"I'll be right over," he teased.

"Kyle, I'm dead tired tonight. Can we get together tomorrow? It's been brutal at the store. Between the swinging door and ringing up customers, I just want some peace and quiet tonight."

"No worries, but I have to tell you, when I think of you in that big porcelain tub, I can hardly contain myself."

She loved when he spoke that way to her. She could feel the heat starting up, and it wasn't from the warm bath water. "Tomorrow, okay?" she whispered into the phone, hating the fact she was turning down a night to be in his arms.

"Okay," he said, a bit crushed. "By the way, Pops wants to know how the wedding plans are coming along."

"Him and my mother both. I need to discuss a few things with you, but I think I have it narrowed down."

"Has she located your dad and brother?"

"No, and that's another thing she mentioned. She suggested that maybe you'd be able to help us find them."

"I'll see what I can do."

"Thanks, baby. I love you."

"I love you, too. Are you sure you don't want me to come over?"

"No, I'm not sure. But if I know what's best, I'll stick to my answer. Let's have dinner tomorrow. I'll fix us something here, and we can talk wedding plans."

He threw himself onto his bed and stared at the ceiling. He'd never felt this much love for another human being—ever. The thought of her soaking in the tub naked had his heart strumming fast. He tried to shake the image out of his head. It was just too difficult. He could clearly envision her smooth skin, piercing blue eyes, and that look she'd give him when she wanted him. He took a cold shower then headed to the kitchen to find something for dinner.

Dirk, exhausted from his first day as short-order cook, was sleeping in his recliner. Kyle walked quietly to the kitchen and peered into the fridge. He should have gotten some of the corn chip pie to go. He shut the fridge and then opened a cabinet. Chicken noodle soup always seemed to work in a pinch. He grabbed the can and a sleeve of crackers and began to make his dinner.

He slurped his soup and crunched on crackers while Dirk snored peacefully in the other room. After his good, yet simple dinner, Kyle moseyed over to the couch where he turned the television on with the sound as low as possible, while still being able to hear it. Every now and then, Dirk stirred. He didn't turn on any lights, and except for the flashes of light from the television, the room stayed dark and perfect for resting. Soon, Kyle's eyes grew heavy, and soon he was keeping rhythm with Granddaddy's snoring.

"Huh, what?" he said, rubbing his eyes and sitting straight up.

"What in the world?" Granddaddy protested, hitting the lever on his recliner and putting the footrest down.

"You two go to bed," Robert said, whistling his way into the kitchen.

Granddaddy furrowed his brows. "Oh, no …"

Kyle looked over at his granddaddy and shrugged.

"He's in love," Granddaddy said.

Kyle swung his feet onto the floor and straightened his back. "Jessica?"

"Who else, boy?"

He shook his head. "I think you need to talk to him. I'm going to bed." He grabbed the remote from the table and turned off the television. "Good night." He shuffled off down the hall to his bedroom.

He crawled under the covers, but before closing his eyes, he looked at the radio alarm clock on the bedside table. He wondered if she was still up and what she was wearing.

"Hey, baby. I know it's late, but I just had to hear your voice one last time before I hit the hay. By the way, what are you wearing?" He chuckled.

"I'm wearing long, flannel pajama bottoms and an oversized T-shirt."

He blinked once, then twice. "Oh."

"Yeah, not exactly sexy bedroom attire, but I have a small crisis on my hands."

He perked up. "What's wrong? Do I need to come over?" He'd jump at the chance to see her, no matter what she had on.

"No. Jessica is here."

He brushed his hand through his hair and sighed. "Yeah, okay. I think I know what that's about. Dad just got home, and he's in a ridiculously good mood. Whistling and everything."

"I'll tell you about it tomorrow, but we may be planning two weddings."

Kyle plopped his head back down on the pillow while holding the phone. "Oh … great," he said.

CHAPTER 24

She was absolutely giddy, and although Becca was dead tired, she listened to her friend. But it wasn't until she heard something about Robert that she really perked up.

"Okay, slow down. What exactly are you trying to tell me?" Becca poured the boiling water into the two cups, covering the tea bags.

"I love him. We're going to get married."

Becca set the kettle down with a thump and turned toward her friend. "You know that sounds totally ridiculous."

"Which part?" Jessica frowned.

"All of it, Jessica. You just met Robert. Not to mention you just moved here and not to mention ..." She blew a strand of hair out of her face.

"That he's older than me?" Jessica arched her brow and then narrowed her eyes.

Becca studied her friend hard. Did she have the strength to hurt her feelings, and was it really necessary? Did it really matter that Robert was almost twelve years her senior? She shook her head a few times. "Yes ... I mean, no. I don't really know." Becca took her mug of hot tea and sat at the kitchen table.

Jessica grabbed her mug off the counter and joined her.

Becca blew on the hot beverage then took a drink. She stared at Jessica from the rim of her cup.

"Say something," Jessica begged.

"I don't know what to say, really. If you and Robert have your minds made up, there's nothing Kyle or I can say to change them. When are you getting married?" She tilted her head, focusing on Jessica's eyes.

"He's been married before, so we were thinking something simple."

"No kidding ... he's been married before?" Becca said with a tone of sarcasm.

Jessica laughed. "We're thinking about maybe travelling to Dallas and getting hitched by the justice of the peace."

"Get hitched? Now you're talking country lingo?" Becca lifted her brows.

"Come on, Becca. Why must you always be the mother hen?"

"I'm not the mother hen. I'm just surprised how fast this turn of events took place. It's one thing if you're enjoying each other … in all the ways a couple does. But then just let that be the anchor that secures your relationship. Why bother with a marriage certificate? Especially since he's—"

"Older?" Jessica finished her sentence.

Becca shrugged then drew the mug to her lips.

"Well, I could ask you the same thing, Becca."

Becca knitted her brows. "How so?"

"You just moved here, you've only known Kyle a short while, and now you're planning your dream wedding. Who is moving fast, now?" Jessica slid her chair back and walked to the kitchen sink, setting her mug down.

"Okay … okay…" Becca sputtered as she gathered her comeback words.

"Okay? That's all you got?"

"I love him. I love him like I suppose you love Robert. So … I'm wrong. There, I said it. You should marry him if that's what feels right. I'll support your decision." She stood and opened her arms.

Jessica rushed into her arms and squeezed her around the waist. "Thanks, Becca. That means the world to me. It really does." She stepped back with her arms wrapped loosely around Becca. "Will you help smooth things over with Kyle and Dirk?"

She nodded. "Leave them to me. I'll get it all smoothed out just fine." She pulled her in for another hug as her mind carefully went over the plans on how to make everything fine.

"I CALLED this meeting today so we can discuss something really important." Becca motioned for both Dirk and Kyle to take a seat at the lunch counter at Full Steam Ahead.

"What's this about?" Dirk looked at Kyle for answers then back to Becca.

"I have to talk quickly. She could come down any moment." Becca tiptoed to see the doorway that led to the upstairs apartment.

Dirk grunted. "Is this about them?" He narrowed his eyes.

"I'm afraid so. Jessica came over last night and poured her heart out to me. I know we may think they're making a mistake, but they are two grown adults, and we have to be supportive of their decision." Becca raised her brows, waiting for disapproval from the men.

"I'm down with it. If Pops is happy, then so am I." Kyle knocked shoulders with his granddaddy.

"Oh, I guess so. But when he comes crying back home cuz it didn't work out, I'll be the one to help pick up the pieces, while you two," he said, flicking his finger at Becca and then Kyle, "are playing house over at the ranch."

"Well, that's the next bit of news." Becca bit her bottom lip before continuing.

"You mean there's more?" Granddaddy said with sheer mockery.

"They want to move in with you." Becca didn't blink a lash as she stared at Dirk.

He turned his finger to his chest. "Me?"

She nodded.

"Now, Granddaddy, think about it for a sec. If both Pops and I move out, that big old house is going to feel pretty lonely."

"True," he whispered under his breath.

"Jessica will keep things lively around there," Becca added.

"So, when are they getting married? Because I don't want them fornicating under my roof without a marriage certificate."

Becca's eyes widened then she covered her mouth to conceal her grin.

THE ANXIETY STIRRED up the butterflies in her stomach, making it difficult to concentrate. She hoped Kyle would understand. She set the table complete with a candle, hoping that would soften any blow as a result of her decision. She checked on their dinner in the oven, a roast chicken with potatoes—the one thing she made really well, and then she opened the bag of mixed greens to make the salad. She uncorked the red wine and decided to sample it before he arrived, anything to help calm the jitters. Just like clockwork, he arrived on time.

"Something smells mighty delicious," he said, sneaking in a kiss.

She cautiously kissed him back.

"What's wrong?" He pulled his head back and peered at her with narrowed eyes.

"Nothing," she said, turning and making her way to the kitchen.

He followed her, spotting the wine. He poured a glass and leaned up against the kitchen cabinets, watching her put the finishing touches to their dinner. "This is pretty good," he said, lifting his glass.

"Yes, I've already sampled it."

"You seem different tonight. What's up, Becca?"

She hated to hear the concern in his voice. This wasn't her intention to put so much doubt in his mind. That was plain crazy. She loved this man. "Let's eat." She pulled the chicken out of the oven and began to carve it.

In the background, soft music played. The flicker of the candle on the table tried to keep beat and did a very good job she noticed. After a few moments of eating in silence, she approached the subject. "About the wedding," she started. "I …"

"I knew it. I knew you weren't acting right. You're cancelling the wedding?"

His dejected demeanor made her feel fragile and she was overcome by an achy feeling in the pit of her stomach. "No, Kyle! That's not it. I've been thinking about the wedding and all the family drama that it will bring—with my mother, and not knowing where my dad and brother are ... and well, I think I just want to do what Jessica and Robert are doing." She puckered out her bottom lip and a tear rolled down her cheek.

"Oh, baby, I'm so sorry I jumped off the deep end." He quickly cupped her hand with his. "If that's what you want, then I'm good with it. I wanted to do whatever made you the happiest. I love you, girl, and I don't care if we get married by a judge or a preacher, as long as we tie the knot." He pushed back his chair and came around to her. Kneeling down while still holding her hand, he stared deeply into her eyes. "You know I love you, baby."

With her free hand she brushed away the trail of tears then chased her blues down with the wine. Choking back emotion like she'd never felt before, she blinked a couple of times before speaking. "What a relief. Thank you for saying all of that. Just like that, I feel all the pressure lifted from me." Her chest heaved as she took a deep breath.

"Okay, so that's settled. We're still getting married and living happily ever after." He smiled as he rose, pulling her up out of her chair.

She circled his rock-hard body and laid her head on his chest, feeling the rise and fall of his breath. "I love you, Kyle."

He pulled her back slightly and lifted her chin with a finger, driving her madly insane with his deep dark eyes and his finely chiseled face. He brushed her hair from her forehead and slid his hand to the back of her head.

"What I feel for you is deeper than love, if that's possible. I dream about you, I think about you every minute I'm awake. Just now, when I thought you were breaking up with me, I was devastated. I wasn't sure what to do." Tilting her head just enough, he moved his mouth to hers, sending her body into a total meltdown.

She clung to his broad shoulders and kissed him back, deepening the kiss and pressing hard against him. He trailed open kisses along the underside of her neck, making her moan softly. "You are so beautiful," he said as he made his way back to her mouth.

His sweet, warm breath lingered just above her lips and it took everything in her not to pull him down on the floor and finish what he'd started—what they'd started.

She threaded her fingers through his hair, settling at the nape of his neck. She clutched a tuft of his hair, gripping it firmly, before running her fingers back through it, making him breathe heavier. "I want you … now," she pleaded in his ear.

He gathered her up into his strong arms and carried her down the hall, while kissing her and bumping into the walls. They finally reached her room where he gently tossed her onto the bed. She landed on her back, the air escaping her lungs, her hair disheveled, and her pulse racing. With her lips parting slightly, she motioned for him to join her.

She'd never seen his face filled with so much tension, his eyes deep and inviting. It made her heart almost stop beating; he was so darn sexy to look at. He tugged his shirt out of his tight-fitting jeans, and quickly unbuttoned it, exposing his tight abs. He pulled off his belt and tossed it aside. Now his jeans, loose at the waist, exposed a bit more to Becca. She gulped quietly, still trying to calm her racing heart. She scooted back on the bed when she realized he was coming closer. He slid in between her legs, and as they came face-to-face, he rolled her over on top of him. He tucked a stray strand of her hair behind her ears, and then taking her face in his hands, pulled her down. Their lips touched lightly at first, and then their kissing increased with intensity.

She pressed a hand to his chest and separated them for a moment. "Kyle …"

He pressed his finger to her mouth. "Shh, no talking." Then he kissed her.

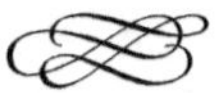

CHAPTER 25

"*L*et me help you with that, Pops." Kyle began to tie his dad's tie.

"I'm super nervous," Robert said, trying to shake off the jitters by rotating his hands at the wrists.

"Just take a deep breath. Remember, I'll be with you." Kyle chuckled and then winked.

"It's been a long time since I've been this happy, Kyle. Jessica makes me feel young again." A smile crossed Robert's face.

"I'm glad, Pops, I really am." Kyle turned his dad toward the full-length mirror. "What do you think?"

Robert admired his son's Windsor knot. "I think your dad is one handsome son of a gun." He squared his shoulders, and tucked in his shirt some more, showing off his trim waistline.

"Well, let's go get those women, and make them our wives," Kyle said, heading toward the door.

"Hey, Kyle," Robert said, stopping him.

"Yeah?"

"I love you, Son. I'm so happy you found Becca. Or rather, she found you. Whichever way it was," he said, stumbling for words. "I want you to be as happy as I was with your mom. She really was the love of my life. I want you to remember that, always." His eyes began to mist.

"I know what you and Mom had was real. That's why I waited until I knew for sure. Do you think Mom would approve of her?"

Robert crossed over to him and placed his hand on Kyle's shoulder. "Not only would she have approved, she'd have loved her like a daughter. And that, my son, is the biggest compliment a daughter-in-law can ever have." He squeezed Kyle's shoulder.

Kyle nodded. "Me and Ms. New York." He threw his head back and laughed.

Robert moved his hand to Kyle's back as they left the bedroom. "Shoot, you and Ms. New York and now me and Ms. New York. Now, that's too funny."

"Ready, Granddaddy?" Kyle asked, putting on his suit jacket.

"Ready as I'll ever be. Where did you say we were going to eat afterwards?"

"It's a surprise," Kyle said, winking at Robert.

"Oh, yeah. Boy, are you in for a surprise, Dad," Robert echoed.

The three men drove to the ranch to pick up Becca and Jessica. The girls had wanted to spend their last night together as single best friends. Kyle wondered if they talked all night and what else they might have done. The three men sat out on the porch, enjoying the fall evening while they drank scotch and smoked cigars. Everyone had their rituals just before they tied the knot—even folks in little towns such as Steam.

"You two look very nice," Granddaddy said to both Jessica and Becca.

"Thank you," Becca said, kissing him on the cheek.

Jessica mimicked Becca, by kissing his other cheek.

Kyle stuck his arm out for Becca. "Ready to get hitched?"

Her eyes twinkled, making his heart race. If he ever thought for just a second he was doing the wrong thing, it totally flew out the window at that very moment. Dressed in a slim fitting navy blue dress, with suede boots that seemed to go on forever, he knew she was the one for him, until death do them part.

Granddaddy sat in the back with the cuddling couple, Robert and Jessica. He stayed scrunched in his corner of the seat and tried to keep his eyes focused on the scenery out his side window.

Kyle drove with one hand on the steering wheel and

the other in Becca's lap. The silky feel of her dress had him on sensory overload.

The ceremony was informal and brief—two couples with Granddaddy as the witness. Once the certificates were signed, sealed, and delivered, they drove to the restaurant. Kyle wasn't sure how that was going to go down. None of them had ever had sushi before.

"What kind of restaurant is this?" Granddaddy asked, looking around.

"Sushi," Robert said, helping Jessica into her chair.

"Sushi! I don't eat raw fish," he said, snapping back.

"Give it a try. There are other items on the menu, if you don't like the sushi. Do you like stir-fry? Rice?" Becca tried to smooth things out with him.

When the rolls came out, Robert, Kyle, and Grand-daddy's eyes all widened.

"What's that?" Robert asked, pointing to little orange round things on the top of one roll.

"Those are called *tobiko*," Jessica explained, picking up a piece with chopsticks and dipping it into her mixture of soy and wasabi. "Also known as fish eggs." She popped the piece into her mouth and chewed.

The sheer expression on Robert's face made Kyle laugh out loud. "Pops, you should see your face."

"I was okay with tempura shrimp, cucumbers and avocado, but then she had to go and ruin it by saying fish eggs." He gingerly took one of the rolls without the orange eggs and placed it on his plate, examining it as if it were going to grow legs and walk away.

"Oh, come on, Robert. Where's your adventurous side?" Becca teased.

Granddaddy seemed quite pleased with his teriyaki stir-fry and rice dish, so all was not a complete failure.

After they left the restaurant, it was a quick trip back home. Kyle was thankful he and Becca were able to convince Jessica they didn't have to go all the way to Dallas to get married by a judge. Warm Springs had that and the sushi restaurant.

"I wish we had more family, Son, to help with all the celebration. But it's just been us for so long," Granddaddy said with a hint of sadness.

Robert reached over and patted him on the leg. "It's okay, Dad. We may be a small family, but we're tight-knit and that's all that matters. Plus, we got Kyle and Becca to make our family bigger. Right, Kyle and Becca?"

Kyle exchanged looks with Becca. "Pops, we just got married. Let us get adjusted to married life before we start talking about kids." He winked at Becca.

He wasn't one hundred percent sure, but he felt like she relaxed her shoulders a bit when he said that. He shrugged then kept driving.

"It's just that we're not having any big reception or any kind of hoopla to celebrate the marriages. In my day, weddings were a big thing."

"Granddaddy, it's okay not to have anything elaborate, but if you really want to plan something, go ahead. Maybe some of the townspeople would be interested." He looked over at Becca to see if she had any reaction.

"That's a great idea, cuz we do have a lot of friends and neighbors," Granddaddy said cheerfully.

Robert and Jessica asked to be dropped off at the apartment first, and then Kyle drove Granddaddy home.

"Do you want us to come in with you?" Kyle asked, realizing how the dynamics had changed for him and so quickly.

"Nah," Granddaddy grunted, getting out of the car.

"Thanks for standing up for us today, Granddaddy," Kyle hollered out Becca's open window.

Granddaddy gave a backhanded wave as he walked up toward the stairs to the porch. Old Duke stood wagging his tail, happy to see him. They watched until he got inside and then drove home.

"Wait," Kyle called out, stopping Becca from moving another step.

"What?" She shrugged then smiled.

"I'm carrying you over the threshold." He pulled her up into his arms.

She circled her hands around his neck and kissed his mouth. "I love you, Kyle Huntsman."

"I love you, too, Mrs. Huntsman."

He juggled her on a knee while he wrestled with the key and the door. Finally, it opened. He shifted her weight in his arms and then proceeded to carry her over the threshold. Once he put her down, the realization of what was to take place took hold of his heart, too.

Before he could say or do anything she reached for him. "Welcome home, Mr. Huntsman." She grabbed him by the tie and pulled him down the hall.

"Wait. Don't I even get a—"

She yanked him once more and their lips touched. She deepened the kiss by pressing hard against him and then teasing him with her tongue.

Muffled words tried to escape through the kiss, but it was of no use. Neither one of them really cared at this point. He lifted her in his arms and carried her to their bedroom.

He held her in his arms as he studied every inch of her face. He noticed highlights in her hair he'd never seen before, and small little laugh lines around her eyes that made him want to kiss each one. He lifted his finger and ran it across her cheek then settling his hands behind her neck, pulled her in closer. "You are so beautiful. I know I keep saying it, but I can't stop." He leaned in and placed a kiss on her lips.

He began to pull back and speak. She pressed a finger to his mouth. "Shh, no talking."

He bent his head and brushed his mouth against hers, a light feathering kiss at first that deepened with desire and fervor typical of any newlywed couple. Without his mouth leaving hers, he lifted his hand and pressed her palm against his chest. His heart was thudding hard against her touch and he pulled back just a tad. "That's what you do to me, Becca," he said, his voice raw and innocent.

She gripped his shirt and pulled him in tighter, closing any space between them. She went up on her toes and pressed her open mouth to his. With a deep groan, he lifted her and together they collapsed on the bed, air exhaling from their lungs.

And then they took their time touching, tasting, and loving every part and every moment of their blissful union as man and wife.

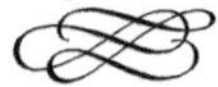

CHAPTER 26

Waking up in his arms was total bliss. The thought that she was now his wife and would be waking up every morning in his arms made her head spin. Rolling over, she snuggled in under his arm. His snoring, smooth and soft, made her snuggle deeper. She reached over and began to twirl the hair on his arms around her fingers, causing him to stir. She moved her fingers to his chest hair and twirled some more. Leaning forward, she kissed his cheek. He stirred even more.

Propping her body up on her elbow, she furrowed her brows. She reached over and ran her finger around the outline of his lips. Nothing. She frowned. She started to roll over the other way when he stopped her. She giggled and rolled into him again. "You weren't really asleep, were you?" She smiled.

"Nope. I was just thinking how lucky I am to wake up every morning with you by my side." He lowered his chin and locked eyes with her.

She rolled her body on top of his and ran her hands through his hair. "That's funny. I was thinking the very same thing."

He rested his hands on her hips, moving her nightgown up ever so slightly. She leaned in and kissed him again. "Well, good morning to you, too," she purred.

"What are we going to do today?" he asked in between small little kisses from her.

"You mean later, right?" She ran her hand along his arms.

"After last night, I'm ready for a big breakfast. You know, pancakes, bacon, and eggs." He laughed as he stopped her hands from moving any lower.

"Kyle Huntsman, are you turning me away?" She rolled off and sighed.

He pulled off the covers and stood near the bed. She looked up at him with narrowed eyes.

"Don't give me that look," Kyle said, pulling her off the bed.

"What? Where are we going?" she said, trying to resist him and his charm.

"I've been dreaming about you in that big shower ever since I laid the first tile. Every time I stuck a tile on the wall, I thought about you. As I glazed grout smoothly over tiles and across seams, I imagined caressing your silky, smooth skin." He led her to the bathroom.

OVER THE COURSE of a few weeks, Dirk Huntsman became the king of the Grill and more. Inventory flew off the shelves, because when folks came in to eat, they always bought something, too. Jessica was constantly reordering items.

"This is so awesome. We're really doing well. I just placed an advertisement in the Warm Springs Daily to let them know about us. I think we'll be getting more customers who just want a different type of experience than what Warm Springs delivers."

"You mean like fast food and fine dining?" Becca laughed.

"Fine dining? You mean the one Italian place with linen tablecloths?"

"Don't forget the sushi place and the steak place."

"I guess. Well, anyway, my point is, more people are going to visit Steam Grill. You wait and see."

"I think that's great. And guess what else is happening here in Steam?" Becca said.

Jessica placed her hands on her hips and raised her brows.

"They are refurbishing the old train depot and

making it a place for visitors to come see. The national park system named it as a historical site!"

"Holy cow, Becca, that's really good news. I can see it now. Businesses will be popping up all over town." Jessica had that faraway look in her eyes.

"I hope not. That's what I like about here. I don't mind the visitors, but they must go home afterward."

"How's married life?" Becca asked Jessica as she did a quick inventory of the shelves.

"Wonderful," she said, glowing.

Becca chuckled. She didn't have to say a word. She knew exactly what she was feeling. "I know. I have to pinch myself to see if it's all real. How's Granddaddy doing with you all there?" Becca jotted down something on a pad.

"He's doing great. I think he really likes us there."

Becca nodded. "I guess Robert has something to tell us. Do you know what that's about?"

Jessica dropped her head quickly, no longer making eye contact with Becca.

"So, you do know what it's about. Give it up, right now, Jessica."

"It's not my place to say."

"Is it bad? Please don't tell me Robert is ill. It—"

Jessica held up her hand. "Stop. No, he's fine. I'm fine, before you go on about that, too."

Becca cut her eyes toward Jessica then knitted her brows. "So, I guess we'll see you tonight for dinner, then."

"Yep, see you then."

"I can't imagine what it is they want to talk about, can you?" Becca tossed a green T-shirt over her head and began to look for some jewelry.

"It had better not be that they want to start a family. I might lose my supper right then and there." Kyle raised his brows and shrugged.

Becca shot him a wild-eyed look. "No way!" She turned to look back at her earring choices.

"I asked if he was ill. She assured me he was fine."

"Maybe it's Granddaddy." Kyle lifted his shoulders, looking worried.

"No, I don't think so. He's been coming to work whistling and seems really good."

"I guess we'll find out soon enough."

"Granddaddy, where do you find the strength to cook all of this after working for several hours over at the Grill?" Kyle slipped his arms around him and squeezed him.

"It's nothing, Son," he said, pulling open the oven door and peeking in.

Over meatloaf, mashed potatoes, and beets he'd

canned from the garden, they chatted about different things.

Then Robert dropped the bombshell. "I'm retiring early next year."

Kyle dropped his fork. "Huh?"

"Yep. Jessica and I want to do some travelling. I could have retired with full benefits at fifty, so I'm going to do it. I'm not getting any younger." He gazed over at Jessica as he cupped her hands.

"What about the Grill?" Becca asked.

"Thought maybe you and Dad could handle it, maybe hire another person or so. When we get back, we'll pitch in and help again." Robert nodded.

"There's not exactly employees lined up here in Steam for jobs, Robert." Becca dug into her meatloaf.

"I'm sure you'll find someone. You're pretty intuitive and creative." His broad smile made everyone smile, too.

"So, what about me?" Kyle finally asked.

"I'm promoting you to Sheriff. Things have been picking up around here since they announced the museum opening, so don't think you won't need a deputy." His father gave him that don't argue with me look.

"As Becca mentioned, it's not that easy finding qualified folks around here."

"That's why I've put out the word to all the neighboring offices ... even in Dallas." He tipped his head and pursed his lips tightly, letting them all know he'd done his part.

"Okay, well I guess that will put my little adventure on hold." Becca took a sip of her iced tea.

Now all eyes were on her.

Her eyes grew wide when she took in all the dropped jaws and surprised looks. She gulped when she figured out they thought she meant something else. She thought fast and quickly eased their minds and to squelch any rumors that would quickly move about town. Holding up a hand to silence the group while vehemently shaking her head she said, "I mean, I'm going…you know, open a gift shop near the new museum." All the ahhs in the crowd let her know she'd disappointed them with her announcement.

"Well, you can just expand the Full Steam Ahead. I think that will be a greatly appreciated addition to the inventory." Jessica laced her arm through Robert's.

"That's a great idea, Jessica!" Becca smiled.

"So, looks like Steam is in for some more changes. I like where we're headed," Granddaddy said.

With dropped jaws, the group looked at Granddaddy.

"You're happy about the changes, Granddaddy?" Kyle arched his brows almost to his hairline.

"Yes, son, of course, I am. Change is good. We have to grow, and part of growing is changing."

Becca cut her eyes to Robert. She wondered if she was the only one finding this new behavior of Granddaddy's strange.

"Glad to hear it, Dad." Robert tipped his head a few times. "Change can be scary, but it can be exciting, too." He patted Jessica's hand still laced through his arm.

"Let's finish eating. I have the best dessert … it came all the way from the grocery store and does not contain any seaweed, raw fish, or fish eggs."

The five of them fell out laughing.

EPILOGUE

Granddaddy Dirk requested help from the townspeople and presented them with a reception anyone would have been proud of. He found more than a few widows able and willing to help decorate and cook. Homemade apple pies and other goodies, along with the best pulled pork and gallons of homemade sauce delighted the partygoers. Pitchers of ice cold lemonade and a keg of beer were provided to wash it all down with, too.

Gifts galore overflowed the gift table and newly printed dollar bills dangled from the money tree. White lights strung from the barn to the house lit up the makeshift dance floor of packed sawdust and rows of folding metal chairs. Everyone enjoyed the music that one of the teens streamed from his new smartphone to two large speakers that were hanging above the dance floor.

The simple wedding cake with white icing and yellow roses, topped with two traditional bride and groom figurines, had everyone licking their fingers because the icing was so good. And instead of a pricy photographer, everyone took pictures with their cell phones and the few disposable cameras that were lying around.

"A good old country reception," Granddaddy sang as he twirled around one of the widows on the dance floor.

In one corner Robert and Jessica snuggled and swayed to a song, and in another corner Becca and Kyle did likewise.

Becca lifted her head from Kyle's shoulder, and looking into his deep brown eyes, she tenderly stated, "I love you so much."

"I have to pinch myself sometimes to see if you're really in my arms," he said, his hands positioned on the small of her back.

"I never thought I'd be able to have a normal relationship," she whispered.

He held her back and stopped swaying. "I told you before. That guy was just plain stupid. He didn't deserve you." He moved her in closer and began to move his hips again, his hard body sending a rippling current through her body.

She stopped moving and put her hand on his chest. "But my parents had something to do with all of that. I mean—"

He cut her off. "One thing we country kids learned at

a very early age is never blame your folks for anything. Only give them credit. So, don't think about all the negative stuff parents do. Cuz you know, babies don't come with a guidebook." He peered down at her then smiled.

"True," she said, moving her hips to the song.

"So what's one positive thing you can say about them?"

They found a seat while the next song played. "This is really hard, Kyle. I always think of the bad stuff." She lowered her head and stared at the ground.

"There must be at least one thing."

"Well, I don't know what I can say about my dad or my brother because they are wanderers, but Mom tried to keep things together. She kept the family house and car, but I don't think she got much support from Dad. She always held a good job, despite their drinking. And come to think of it, after Daddy left, Mom slowed way down on her drinking."

Kyle took her hand in his and squeezed it. "See? So there were some good memories. They were just hidden."

"Probably because of all the other crap that I dealt with," she said.

"I think after things settle down, you should invite your mom out here. See if you can put things back on course."

She threw her hands around his neck excitedly and hugged him. "See? This is why I love you."

His lips brushed against hers, sending waves of excitement through every fiber of her being. She could feel her cheeks begin to blush as the warmth spread.

"I always wondered if I'd meet the girl of my dreams. Never knew she was hiding out in New York all this time, or I'd have made a trip out there." His smile was infectious.

Grinning, Becca nodded. "I know, right? If I'd thought that my guy was sitting on a porch somewhere in Texas, rocking his life away, I would have come out here sooner, too."

"Speaking of rocking chairs …" He tossed his big arm around her shoulders and urged her to walk with him. "I've been eyeing a pair over at the hardware store in Warm Springs."

She raised her chin and gazed lovingly into his warm eyes. "Get five. I have a feeling we'll be having visitors."

STEAM LOVED THEIR LAW ENFORCEMENT. Even though the population of Steam was quite small compared to other towns, the outlying areas required law and order, too. They felt safe with having father and son guarding the town. So, when it came time for Robert's retirement ceremony, it also came with lots of flowing tears—the good kind. The kind when you're happy for someone and all that they've achieved.

When Robert turned and pinned the big Sheriff

badge on Kyle's shirt, even Robert's eyes misted. "Congratulations, Son." Robert pulled him in for a man hug.

"Speech," several people cried from the crowd.

Kyle walked up to the podium in the community room of the church. He gathered his thoughts for this very impromptu speech. "Dad," he said, as his eyes met his father's. "Becca," he nodded toward her as she sat clearly emotional from the day's service, "and community members," he said, scouring the crowd. "Thank you for being part of this very emotional and grateful day. I'm glad my dad is retiring and doing some things he's always wanted. I'm also very grateful for the opportunity to serve the great town of Steam."

The crowd applauded.

He cleared his throat and continued. "You see, since I was a boy, I've always wanted to serve and protect. I thought about joining the military, but when I got a glimpse of my granddaddy and my father doing the job that Steam hired them to do, I thought I also would make a great team member. I don't know how many of you recall, but I started out riding my bike through the streets of Steam looking for crime. I'd ride my bike as fast as I could to report it. Back then, it was kids tossing rocks at glass windows, or smoking in the dry weeds, which is a serious fire concern in our summer heat, to even reporting the occasional elderly person needing assistance. Our crimes are still little and most of the time insignificant, but we all know that crime can come into small towns and we must always be vigilant. And now, with the museum, we are seeing an influx of tourists and others, so let's all do our part in keeping Steam happy, healthy, and safe for all of our residents. Thank you for your support." He stepped away from the mic.

More cheering and applause came from the crowd.

Stretching his body toward the mic, he grabbed hold of it again. "One more thing. There are refreshments in the back thanks to the ladies' auxiliary. Thank you, ladies. Please help yourself."

In the crowd, you could hear some giggles coming from the ladies' auxiliary members. Then the crowd of about thirty-five people disbursed to the back of the room to get iced tea and cookies.

Life in Steam moved at an extreme pace even for Steam. If Becca hadn't seen it with her own eyes, she'd not have believed it. The Steam Train Depot Museum brought tourists in by the carload, and with the handy new fliers she had made up, many of them ended up at the Full Steam Ahead Grill.

Becca and Kyle heard from Robert and Jessica in the form of postcards with very few words on them. They envied their travels to Spain, Italy, and more, and counted the days until they'd be back. In the meantime, the five rocking chairs sat ready and waiting on the front porch of their new house.

Old Duke crossed the Rainbow Bridge while Robert and Jessica were gone. He'd had a great life out on the ranch. And to keep Dirk on his toes, Kyle and Becca got him a little something … you know, to help ease his pain of losing old Duke.

Granddaddy laughed like a schoolboy while the little black and tan shepherd pup licked his face. "Now, you stop it, Ranger," he said, laughing so hard he wheezed.

"Isn't he the cutest thing ever?" Becca reached for Ranger.

"He's a little spitfire," Granddaddy said, brushing some of the little hairs from Ranger off his shirt.

"He needs obedience training," Kyle said, shaking his head.

"He's just a pup," Granddaddy protested.

"Yeah, Kyle." Becca held the little puppy up to her face, and he licked her earlobe, making her giggle.

"Well, I'm glad you think he's cute." Kyle winked then took off down the steps and around the corner of the old ranch.

Becca wrinkled her brows at Granddaddy.

Granddaddy shrugged. "Don't look at me."

Becca's eyes grew expeditiously in size when she saw Kyle coming around the back of the house holding another pup—a black and tan puppy that looked identical to Ranger.

"Kyle Huntsman," she said with a sound of warning in her voice.

"I couldn't leave him there. He was the last one. He's the runt." He held him up for her to get a good look. Ranger started kissing his brother and the two became rambunctious. She set Ranger down and the two started chasing each other.

"What are we going to do with a pup?" Her hands were on her hips.

"Same thing I'm going to do," Granddaddy said.

Becca cut him a look. "We're both working … a lot." She smirked.

"They have these things … they're called pee pads. They work like a charm." Granddaddy laughed out loud.

She blew a burst of air out of her lungs. "Well … he is cute," she said, watching the pair play. "What shall we name him?"

"I don't know. You're the creative one," Kyle said, watching the pups chase their tails and wrestle.

Becca held up her hand. "I got it. I got the perfect name for him."

"Well, girl, spit it out," Granddaddy said.

"Chief."

"Chief," both men said at the same time.

"I like it," Kyle said, looking at the pups. "What's for dinner, Granddaddy? I'm starving," Kyle said.

Granddaddy stood and made his way toward the creaky old screen door. "I got some pork chops smothered in gravy, mashed potatoes, and cornbread, Son. Come on in and stay for a while."

Kyle reached down and grabbed little Chief while Becca rounded up Ranger, and then they followed Granddaddy into the charming old ranch house that held a lot of great memories for her. She recalled the first time she'd had supper with them. Becca knew then they would become her extended family. She watched as Kyle helped his Granddaddy get things going in the kitchen. Her heart throbbed for this man every day. She was so happy she'd taken that assignment two years ago, bringing her to Steam, Texas.

Debbie currently lives near Charleston, South Carolina with her husband and one rescue dog. She's passionate about animal rescue and as such donates a percentage of all her book sales yearly to an animal rescue organization. She loves to connect with readers, so don't be shy. Sign up for her newsletter at www.authordebbiewhite.com

Ties That Bind

Passport To Happiness

The Missing Ingredient

The Salty Dog

The Pet Palace

Billionaire Auction

Billionaire's Dilemma

Coaching the Sub

Christmas Romance – Short Stories

9 781736 380307